BOGEY BONHOMIE

to My friends
"On earth's paradise,
some suffer what they like.
I love what I do,
And I live and will die for it."

sun:jeev
©opyright Material

@sunjeevbhatia on Instagram

BOGEY BONHOMIE

BOGEY

BONHOMIE

A friend in deed, is a friend indeed.

Cover illustration & design : Preet Soni ©anada
Inside Illustrations : Sun:Jeev & Drishti Balani
Novel story ©Copyright Sanjeev Bhatia(India)
Title B O G E Y B O N H O M I E ©COPYRIGHT sun:jeev

15.2993degree N, 74.1240 degree E (Goa Latitude and Longitude)

Picture below G O A Airport (2024)

'Friendship is a matter of great latitude, for it to have any longitude.' - sun:jeev ©

A (fore)word on Bonhomie.

The thing in friendships, is that friends talk loosely. It is the nature of the relationship, to allow each other a sense of abandon and freedom.

They say things. To each other.

They do things. Together.

Sometimes, in a manner, of *a figure of speech.*

Some mean it, some don't.

Some are just mean.

Friendship, is more than just something you can put up in a *figure of speech*.

You have to show up, you have to be consistently there for each other, you have to show intensity even after years of an interval. A gap does not mean, it is over.

You cannot divorce a friend.

You have to be there in action, in *spirit*. All your life.

Not just in thoughts, but also in deeds.

It should be fun. Friends forget looking at the time, when in best company.

That defines bonhomie. If this book was about that, then it would be as simple as this one page.

Clean, genuine, simple and fun.

This story however, is everything but that.

Rationality is sometimes missing in relationships between some friends who started as rivals, even just acquaintances.

Then it just goes south from there.
South Goa that is.

In some cases, it is intended to be that way, a bogey, a pal who turns out to be your bugbear. Such that even a trustworthy friend cannot save the friendship.

Only angels can save friends, when the friendship is lost.

Now that makes this a more interesting story – that is the story of Bogey Bonhomie.

Enjoy the read.
Like the friend, be on the right side of your friends,
like the written words on this page.

It makes life living better, before and in after life.

You are born into a family,
friends you choose,...or maybe they have chosen you.

CONTENTS

& ... Page #

PART 1 - 1961 Echo from Goa

1. Twilight ...13
2. Half a day ago ...18
3. Fiend and Friend ...25
4. Punishment for Loyalty ...33
5. Confession of a Paadri ...42

PART 2 - The re-incarnation

6. Picnic & Monkey Pranks ...50
7. A Monkey in Bed ...67
8. Self interest in College ...74
9. Time Pass. Time, passes ...80
10. Downhill ...93
11. Letters over the years ...108
12. The Final call ...121
13. Sept. 10^{Th} 2007 ...125
14. E~Mail ...129

15. Sarkaar's Diary ...134
16. Kuber : In transit ...155
17. The Reply ...163
18. You cannot refuse ...171
19. Journey to Goa ...177

PART 3 ~ THE BOGEY

20. The trap ...190
21. Deja Vu ...198
22. The unfathomable loss ...203
23. A broken man ...208
24. Kuber's predicament ...212
25. Penultimate ...220
26. Nightmare ...233

PART 4 ~ THE BONHOMIE

27. Soul Searching ...245
28. Dinshaw's Day off ...252
29. Friendly Angelic Ghost ...262
30. The jump ...275
31. Song of Sid and Ray's Ghost ...282

PART – 1.
The echo from Goa

(1961)

1961 Echo from Goa

'I make you an offer, you can't refuse.'

'I make you an offer, you can't refuse.'

'I

make

you

an

offer,

you can't refuse.'

Illustration:
The above is an
Understatement figure of speech, that
makes something seem less serious, less
bad, than it really is.

An introduction to Ray & Roy.

This is not just another friends story, one buried in the sands and the southern island of Goa.

It was of a time, when there was no bridge over the Mandovi, and the Portuguese were beating a hasty retreat, burning down even small bridges.

It was a friendship getting buried with history. It was 1961, on an evening in Goa that India won it's liberation from Portuguese rule.

Till then, it had been a story of Roy Lobo and Ray Noronha with bonhomie at it's centre.

The one, between two friends, Ray and Roy, known as Ra-Ro in the fishing village of Palolem, South Goa. A time, when sand was golden, the sea's surf was pure white, and the water bluer than the sky.

Ray a devout Jesus follower, sought God in all things. He wore the cross on his chest in a blue-black ink that was tattooed right down from his neck to the sternum, down to his navel. The shorter, upper horizontal bar of the cross, was marked on his clavicle – the collar bone, right till the edges of his humerus.

Roy Lobo did not wear any cross on his chest. Not even in a thread or chain of steel. 'Jesus bore enough for us all, by wearing it on his back,' would be his oft repeated comment of Ray's cross. Each time they played football, and Ray would be without his shirt, he would only wear a set of beads in his neck. 'He look like a marked boy from Jesus, the son, of the son of God.'

'*Deed over speech my friend*!' would be the only retort from Ray.

Roy never had a repartee to that. He loved Ray. A bit too much. At least that is what Ray thought. Ra-Ro were a pair, right from their Jesuit school days.

From the days when chapels were still being built in every kilometre for the village community. From the days of Father Varghese listening to everyone's confessions at Sunday Church. Yet they prayed differently.

Ray visited only Father Varghese's church, and Roy frequented every chapel within the community. Roy was keen to meet people in different neighbourhoods. Until that fateful evening, when they took the wind-surfing aerial route, on Roy's insistence.

'I make you an offer Ray, you can't refuse.' That is all Roy Lobo said, and took Ray Noronha off-balance, off-guard.

1. Epigram

A figure of speech, like a brief saying, introducing antithetical ideas exciting surprise and attention.

Illustration:
'I made no friend, when all I try, is never to make a foe.'

1. Twilight

A slow mother turtle trudges toward the edge of the waves breaking on the beach. It hides its head inward, as the leathery dome shell, barely covers its thick hind legs. A dozen primates zip forward into the flat sea low tide, side-stepping the scared reptile. The child like apes *gecker* as their mothers scream with them on their backs. The darkness on the beach, results in a troop of the monkeys taking a leap to ricochet off the back of the scared reptile.

The turtle head, remains firmly concealed inside it's shell.

The tirade of macaque noise, their tail thumping and hand-like foot movement around the herbivore cryptodira causes the reptile to flutter in fear. It's carapace quivers while its scales appear like the sand the scales merge with. Yet each time, the monkeys appear to have left, and the turtle bobs its head out, it hides its head back in, leaving it's wing like forearms splattered flat in the sand.

As twilight breaks out, and the tiny tots have been reunited with their mother monkeys on the sand-bar between the sea and the *Canacona Island*, the *Palolem* bred turtle begins it's infinite attempt to complete the walk it had commenced in the evening. It is weary, with it's new born in company. The new born has unearthed life from under the sand. It has been lying under since two months. The mother turtle, protective in paranoid maternal instinct.

The nearby sea looks further away, as it still believes it can enter the water before dawn, hoping to ride the tide. It's baby turtle joins another troupe, swept away with the tide.

Canacona's Monkey Island, is the island in the middle of the sea, overlooking the Palolem Goan beach, and is still going to be a further swim for the rock like turtle to end it's journey. As it crawls past small footprints of the father monkeys walking confidently into the sea, the rocky turtle stops at the head of a human it has mistaken for a hairy coconut shell.

Ray Noronha lay wet on the beach, half his face inside the moist sand. He can see from one eye, listen from one bleeding ear and barely breathe from one sand blocked nostril. Like the turtle, Ray has his head pitted on one side of his rubbery neck. He silently gazes into the eye of the turtle. The turtle merely looks back quietly. His legs break ripples in the foamy waves as the Arabian Sea fills up the flares of his pants. Both appear as lifeless to the other, as each judges the life options and path ahead.

The mother turtle shares the grief of sudden parting with its baby, with Ray with a glum look.

Ray's left arm is broken, his neck twisted, with a bloody tear pouring out from his eyelids, across his nose entering his wet collar behind the neck.

The pose makes him look like a cripple posturing for sleep to the reptile who is still confused between hiding, continuing his journey and gawking.

The early morning sunrise creates a glistening radiance on his face, as much as it makes the turtle look greener than brown.

Ray wants to be relived off his pain, and blinks appealing for some shut eye to the turtle. Ray has spent over six hours on that deserted spot, the same that the turtle has taken to plod to this edge of the sea, where human meets shell.

Ray tries to move his arm, which the turtle quickly avoids to move away from the potential trapping embrace.

Toward the inland, the music has finally died out two hours ago. Ray had been listening to the musical repeat of 'Ya Ya, Maya Ya' in his left ear, while the right side remained embedded in the *Palolem* beach, filling up sand in his ear canal up till the ear-drum.

He was afraid he would no longer be able to listen to his favourite Goan rhythm, nor participate in the Portuguese dance he was so accustomed to partake in with the girls at his favourite beach. He could now barely peer over to see light hit the colourful shacks, the figurine of which he had tried to stare at, keeping him awake through the night.

Had he been at the centre of the crescent shaped beach, some form of life would have perhaps found him. Unfortunately he lay at the deserted spot angled away from the large rocks and palm trees near the shacks, a sort of no-man's reptile and monkey path land.

It was ironical, that his ribs lay broken, while those of the new turtles, belonging to the order testudines, were safely crawling away rib-caged with their shells. The only similarity with ribbed humans, you loose your shell, as a turtle, you lose your skeleton and you die. Ray was minutes away from his end.

He hoped like his youth, some young boys come to play footie-ball opposite the archipelago.

'I made no friend, when all I try, is never to make a foe.' Ray reflects.

The parasailing balloon he had fallen off from was stuck on the northern shoreline swaying coconut trees. From the turtle sand view, the balloon looked like a red sky-high shack in mid-air, where only the coconuts could party. Ray's safety harness was still strapped on to his soaked beach-shirt. His turtle-shell, a robe like coconut fibre matte like net, was not going to save him. The turtle looked bemused.

'What a great plan Roy Lobo!' was all Ray could mumble. The mother and other baby turtles crawl by, seeming disinterested as soon as they see a form of noise and life ebb in Ray. They begin the slow swim into the tide going out.

The new mothers had left lighter leaving their eggs deposited in the moist sand behind the rocks at night, and had hoped to ear mark the spot near the red balloon and the palm trees. The older mothers awaited their progeny to swim into the shallow sea water to be reunited with their female babies. Global warming had done away with the male babies, more prone to survive in colder sand upon hatching.

Ray had decided to get air-borne with much chagrin; relying on Roy whom he had doubted all his school and '*fishy*' life.

Tears of blood flooded his only working eye few inches above the sandy beach. One sealed eye had been frozen close by the dried blood clots below his eyebrow, and the only working eye looked like it was gazing through red glass.

The parasailing balloon looked even more mercurial.

2. Personification

A figure of speech that attributes human characteristics to something that is not human, or not for a person.

Illustration:
Fear hugged him like a friend, in it's grip, it filled Lobo up with more anger. (Fear is given a personal quality)

2. Half a day ago...
(12 hours back)

'No Roy Lobo, I am not cut out for this,' spoke a distressed Ray trying to save himself.

'Nice beach type *camisa* you wear men. When you will fly ova-the sea then? I will be behind you, and Drake is in the boat below. Not to worry ya.'

Ray retorts immediately 'This height is not for me, water no problem.'

'Drake expert boatman, why you worry. Me with him in boat too. Cun-men, I challenge you. I beat you at it, one pao, chourico and I top it off with...Ginjinha. '

'Me happy with torrad pao and port. Understand no..., Ma will be upset with you again.' Ray warns.

'You and your bread-toast. You go toasted from Gova man. Bloody *Chamucas*' fires Lobo.

'It is '*samusa*' man. Ma will fry you.'

'You are my *irmao manus*, Ray Noronha. My *bradder*. I promise *Tio Noronha.*'

'No brother no primo. Jus' friends, no alcool amigo. Lemme worry about Ma,' replies Ray.

'You see, this fear from heights must go, else how you will bring down coconuts for *Tio Noronha?* See you feat football first, we fight off the fear.'

'Look Roy Lobo, I never say to your dad, why he call himself Mr. Lobo when he be a *Churi-Gaonkar*. Sell your knives no, why sell these balloon coco rides? '

'My cachola, my cabeca, don't tell me what I can sell or what I cannot sell. You the British now?'

There is silence between the two amigos.

Roy continues to persuade, 'Look Ray Noronha, we fear, we finish. The Portuguese leave anytime now. It not be 1950. it waz the 1961 now. We lose ten years man, we lose another ten, it be the nineteen seventy one and we become ol'men.'

'First be good man. I tell you from school, to learn *the proper* English. You no listen. No, never.' Ray is exasperated.

'What to learn men, first the English go away now the Portuguese go any day. We only have to live in Chacha Nehru land. Old man not want any Portuguese here men, what the point to learn English, my Konkani better. I only live in Guvaa. How do I care? If the Spanish come next, I go away to Monkey Island.'

'Anyways you not a monkey Lobo, you Churigaonkar. The knife man. Cut open the coco coccus.' The junior Noronha knows, he is the main support to his mudder. His ma will be mad at Roy and Ray, if they caught breaking their own coconuts.

'Hey hey, I put my knife in your back a-what? I teach you to fly. Later many year, I be in boat and you in air. We be a team from school. You my *kuker and gurf* men.'

'I no spoon and fork, you sure the knife though. I tell you to be straight from school days...but you no listen.' Ray realized how his English language suffered as did his Portuguese at the hands of his pal Roy Lobo.

The village knew them as Ra-Ro, as they were inseparable from school in 1949, to the beaches now in 1961, at the cusp of Goa's liberation.

Ψ

If only Ray had been a bit separated, he would not be lying with a bloody eye, and a blood clotted one at Palolem beach that dawn of 1961. Little did he know then, that the Indian Army would march into Goa, and overthrow the Portuguese.

Ray Noronha bled to death on that *Palolem* beach remembering his conversations with his friend, who he wanted to make good.

That is all he wanted; he wanted Roy Lobo to be a good man. In the bargain, he missed living his own life properly.

As life ebbed in Ray at *Palolem* beach, twilight took the turtle trudging into the sea, while the monkeys jumped off to Monkey Island. It was where Roy Lobo hid in fear. Fear hugged him like a friend, in it's grip, it filled Lobo up with more anger.

Lobo was sitting below a clump of trees at Monkey Island, staring at a tribe of them jump up and down the tree, chasing each other's tails.

Roy Lobo had not bathed, eaten or talked to anyone socially since thirty six hours in hiding. His facial twitch resembled the troop of mammals.

He wondered, if he was reborn as a monkey, would he have preferred having a tail. His body had the same fur like androgenic hair on his chest and back, and surprisingly grey grizzly hair graced his butt and legs.

He had always aped Ray, and now lost him forever. Fear filled him up, after his planned attempt to disengage Ray from the air gliding operation, he wondered how the local police and the changed administration would consider him. 'Am I the murderer, am I the criminal they hunt for?'

The coconut fibre had all come off, and the netting of the fishing boats, had not been light enough and yet not sturdy enough to hold Ray up in the air after his take off. Roy was filled with remorse and tears swelled up in his eyes.

Roy Lobo, watched as the primate mammals plucked the *Zapote* nearest to their arms, a Spanish fruit known as *Chickoo* in *Hindoostaan*. The colour of the fruit resembled the mammals natural skin and fur, and hundreds of monkeys now jointly feasted on it like a ceremonial lunch.

Lobo gazes at the tribe of monkeys, surprised at their team work and jointness. Their cohesiveness appears to him as if they represent a family. They glide down from the tree staring back at him, some hopping from the vines directly landing near his feet.

The two sets of primates, feel the invasion of their privacy by a pirate looking grizzly, resembling an ape, but with clothes partly torn, partly covering his fairer skin.

The tribe watching Lobo curiously, back resting against another Zapote tree, grows suspicious.

Lobo at that instant, acts in his usual instinctive self. He picks up three round shaped stones, and throws them at a tree bark, nearby to where the monkeys stand. He hopes that the macaques follow and mimic the same action, tossing some *chickoos* toward his hungry self.

The monkeys with mouth and cheek pouches filled with the delicious fruit, take the unkind action poorly. They first run to hide behind the tree they descended, making noises in a collective opera to get the attention of their friends on the branches above. The jungle comes alive with their cacophony.

They own their space. After all, it is Monkey Island, out of Guva's village limits. There's no Portuguese, there are no Indians.

Another hundred monkeys descend from nearby trees and look toward the injured pride of the hurt monkeys hiding behind the *chickoo* filled Sapota tree.

A large male macaque, with its long face, chews out the seed of the *Sapote*, spits it out toward the grass below the tree it had hidden behind, and picks up two stones with both its long furry arms. His entire tribe and the century of monkeys that have now descended into the forest, closing in on the fearful Lobo imitate the large macaque.

Roy Lobo, winces in the preparation of the pain about to be inflicted upon him. He quickly estimates over two hundred stones that are about to be flung at him. He has time to recollect his own naughty mischievousness that had made him fling down Ray at the football match outside his school hillock, atop the garden.

The macaques all take aim, and replicate the action taken by Lobo – who brings it upon himself to embody the bark of the tree against which he rests. Every monkey of the forest now throws a stone at that tree trunk and torso of Roy Lobo.

As they inch nearer and nearer and take aim, the probability of their connection with a part of Lobo's face and chest increases infinitely, bloodying him and his features beyond recognition. Initially the macaques enjoy the blood sport.

After a while, each scoring *macaque* walks away, with a bored expression on it's face. Many scratch their heads in disinterest after having taken aim. 'What is with these humans?'

'Don't they understand mother nature? You don't try to fly in the air and take pot-shots on trees.'

As Lobo becomes a target practice scarecrow, he remembers his own monkey like pranks on the footie-ball field.

3. Oxymoron

Oxymoron is a figure of speech that combines two contradictory ideas or words, that are said and used in the same statement.

Illustration:
He is inhuman and truly deceptive. A fiend and a friend at the same time.

3. Fiend and Friend

'**R**oy Lobo, I have to finish my studies. I cannot play.' Ray is exasperated, as Lobo never takes no for an answer.

'Arrey, you fight me men, like the Marathas fought the Portuguese. I am your *Mitra*, your Irmao, your Braddar man. How Braddar will play footie-ball without my *axepert, prefect, braddar on da other side?*'

Ray remains silent.

Roy Lobo pleads again, 'You will be noticeably absent on the field, and all the friends will keep talking about you, when you are not *dhere. Why be here, rather than dhere?*'

'Okay, I will be *there*! Give me five minutes, now go.'

'I love to hate you men.' Lobo shouts, as he leaves Ray's room.

For want of saying anything else, Polly Coelho puts in his two bit, following Lobo outside, 'I love to beat him man. We beat him, we win big.'

Happy Dias chips in, 'You beat Ray, you impress the village girls. All the *meninna fofa*, the *garrrota linda* see us as bigger man.'

Roy Lobo chips in, 'Not easy to beat his footwork man, not easy to beat him on dance floor, not easy to beat him before the girls. They all want to do '*maya ya, Ya ya mayaya*' with him only. Not easy to make him play, when he know he nevva' lose.'

'*Mhaka naka go, naka go*, we must beat Ray Noronha!' Polly is all charged up.

'You take care Polly. Move your footy, not your polly on the field then,' reprimands Roy. 'Not to kick like last time, to tackle, dribble, possess and pass.'

The garden outside the school atop the hill hock, is few minutes walk from their homes.

Sam D'silva and Ray Noronha live on the middle class side of the colony closer to the beach. They walk daily together toward the garden, a patch of grass sloping away from the beach. It faces monkey island and the archipelago on the other side, with open land getting in sea waves in slow ripples and slight winds. It makes for a scenic yet peaceful place to play.

At the bottom of the hill, are cemented stone chairs which are behind the makeshift goal post that the boys have created by tying a fishing net between two coconut trees.

Sam, is on *Ray's side of the turf* choosing to shoot downward the hill, so that they get less tired. With each other for company they know they can keep control and possession of the ball for longer time, and will not have to defend going upward. Sam is *Ray's loyal friend*, genuinely on the foot ball field and the field of life too.

'I just love to love you man. You are the only friend, who walked with me to school all these years. Now you picks me up on your cycles on the way to schools. These rich fellows don't see the difficulties we see all the times, any times.'

Ray replies, 'Pick you on my cycle Sam. Anytime Sam, not *anytimes*. Singular buddy.'

Sam ruefully retorts, 'I say the same you are my single friends.'

'Friend Sam, friend' corrects Ray.

'Same thing.' grins Sam.

'Well Sam, actually we are all friends, we will be there at different times, different places and be there for each other someday.'

'Ray, only friend, different time, same place. I will be your only friend. Singular Ray not plulal.'

Ray smiles at the toothy Sam. 'Plural, Okay, never mind Sam, Lets kick some ball.'

'Some balls and arses too. Plulal Ray, Plulal.' winks Sam.

The footie game starts, with Lobo, Polly and Happy on one side and Sam, Ray with the beach bum Drake on the other. Drake never attends school as he is a keen oarsman for fishermen. He's older yet less skilled, so they keep him as their goal-keeper. Happy defends the Polly and Lobo goalpost.

Lobo acting like the moron he likes to be, kicks the footie ball hard, toward Sam, hitting him below his belly. Sam doubles up in pain, and Lobo runs off laughing, 'See you broken balls after the match, save your shins Sammy. I *torrad* your balls.'

'Your *kobi tomates*!' Sam abuses looking toward Roy Lobo, bent over himself. He can think of tomatoes and cabbage even in pain.

Ray makes Sam bend and heal, so that they can start again in a few minutes with the conceded foul. Both Ray and Sam dribble beating Polly easily, as Lobo attempts to catch hold of Ray's tee-shirt to slow him down.

Ray scores with precision and in a few minutes they lead 3-0. The possession of the ball remains with Sam and Ray all the time.

The next round of attack and Ray is running downward the slope to score a fourth. As he nears the goal-post, Lobo sticks his leg out at a speedy Ray, who trips over Lobo's shin, and goes flying toward the concrete stone chairs behind the fishing net goalpost.

Ray lands on to the chair seat surface, his pelvic bone hitting the stone, and his knee trapped below the stone surface of the chair. Sam on the other side can see the foul clearly, and runs angrily at Lobo, who runs to hide behind Polly for cover.

Ray lies bundled up in pain, unable to get up. As minutes pass, Lobo runs off, laughing toward the beach. Drake, Polly and Sam rescue Ray, lifting his crumpled body, and carry him on their shoulders to his house. Happy carries his shoes, and the footie-ball they use to play.

Ray is now indisposed for weeks at home, as he bleeds repeatedly in his urine. Only Drake, Sam and Harry come over daily to visit him.

'That ape of a boy, is a dunce or a gorilla, we do not know, but do not let him come anywhere close to my son. You must play with your age group.' Happy and Sam are staring at their feet.

Ray looks up from his bed, 'Sam why you tell Ma?' 'Ma, Drake has nothing to do with it.'

'Auntie, it was deliberately done by Lobo.' Harry speaks up. 'I was in his team, but knew not, not know... his, his intention. He stammers.

Drake is silent.

Sam fills in, 'He is inhuman and truly deceptive. A fiend and a friend at the same time.'

Drake speaks up looking up at Ray's mother, 'I am sorry Tia, my fault, my fault. I never listen to Ray, I always listen to Roy due to *masti*. We only want to have fun, but Ray have fun and work hard also. So Ray, really full life, he be a full man.'

Ray Lobo's mother looks on at Drake and Sam with a sad expression.

'No be sad Tia. Roy Lobo not a fair man. Ray Noronho is a good friend and a good man. I sit here with him, even if it takes few weeks and months, you go Tia, you go, you do your kitchen work, you cook for your son, you make him okay. We tend to him. Not to worry. Ray have us all. We, all of us we be - his best friends, because *Ray never referentiate.*' Drake is all pumped up emotionally.

You mean difference..' supports Sam.

'Differentiate. Chips in Ray.

'I mean, he no need referee. He love us all. He dooz for us all.' says Drake dryly.

'He does...not dooz' corrects Ray again. Tia puts her hand over Ray's mouth, and gesticulates to him to sleep.

All of them break into peels of laughter. Tia puts her hand on Drake's shoulder and accepts his support.

'Now our turn Tia our turn.' Polly has tears in his eyes, as he walks closer to Ray. 'We be with our man,...you go cook for the night.'

This cools Ray's mother seething anger, while Ray can only manage a weak smile. He barely turns, flinches in pain, and almost immediately falls asleep, leaving his friends standing there, fussing over him.

Ray flies and soars in his dream-world; he can imagine wearing Roy's make-shift coconut fibre parachute balloon in his dream....he can see himself fly. How can he refuse to fly?

He recollects the time when he was in school and some of these friends were his daily companions.

Ray Noronha and Roy Lobo's school in South Guva (Goa)

4. Antithesis

A figure of speech, that strongly states contrasting ideas, placed in juxtaposition.

Illustration:
Ray had become the bugbear to Father Varghese and the bete-noire to Lobo, yet he was an angel to Drake and Happy, and the soul mate to Sam.

4. Punishment for Loyalty

There is a din in the corridor outside all the grade IX and X class-rooms.

As the vice principal of the school, father Varghese wonders, why a small delay from him has caused this commotion in his Moral Science class room. 'These kids go berserk really quickly,' he mutters as he hurriedly takes steps towards the class.

There are paper rockets flying over the front-benchers.

Paadri Varghese walks into the class, which is the source of the pandemonium and single handedly picks out Ray upon entry. 'Ray Noronha, step aside here!'

The classroom of mischievous, naughty and pesky boys had quietened down seeing the Paadri approach the class from the long corridor, something Ray has no liberty to watch, as he was at the black-board. His back was turned away from the door entry of the classroom.

Ray funnily had wiped off all the names he had written on the black-board, since the students had quietened down seeing the Paadri about to enter the class.

This led to letting go off lightly all the trouble makers, despite numerous warnings to the rule-breaking students, some of who are his best pals during the recess break. Not wanting them to get into trouble, he actually protects them, without realizing that the Paadri at the door is suspiciously watching his action of rubbing off the white chalk names, with the duster.

It all happens in a flash, simultaneously.

One of the students, Happy, who has his back turned, is belting out Polly, with his leather belt, slapping it on the desk which Polly hides under. The Paadri shouts and admonishes Happy, who drops the belt immediately. He is so scared, that his loose pants fall off.

Father Varghese is brutal in his punishment, 'You, Stand on the desk right away.' He clicks his tongue, 'No no, leave the pants. Stand in your underwear so that the entire class can see your skinny legs and bony bum, you, you, scoundrel.'

Walking over the desk, he pulls out Polly, from under the desk, pinching his ears, 'Why were you hiding?' Behind him he finds Roy Lobo

'Sir, sir, you can see Happy was attacking me.' Roy does not relish a punishment, and dishonestly parks the blame on Happy, not re-telling how he has poked him with his compass, torn his copy books, and tied his school bag loose cloth handle into knots.

Father Varghese loudly admonishes Ray before the entire class 'You are supposed to stand in for Xavier sir. Unable to manage the class, what kind of Prefect are you? We wanted you to be the head-boy of the entire school next year! How will you help run the senior school when you cannot manage a class?'

Ray goes red in the face, like the colour of tomato ketchup falling all over his cherubic face. Ray wrings his hands, and looks down at his polished black shoes. A bead of sweat breaks out over his lip, as his pencil thin meagre moustache looks darker than usual, with it's wetness of embarrassment.

Father Varghese picks on Sam next. He questions him to reveal names of the naughty boys in class.

Sam does not move. He places his textbook before his stomach and pants. His school shirt is pulled out of his pants. Father Varghese is perplexed.

'Fold your shirt inward,' shouts Father Varghese. The boy does not react to the Paadri's orders.

Sam expresses the same awkwardness with which he as an assistant prefect, or any other student would stand with his erection in his short-pants, covered with a text book, when a teacher would summon them suddenly to inspect their copy books.

The Paadri's reprimand had caught Sam napping, more than his adolescent imagination ever had. There was no relaxing of his erection, despite the pressure from the Paadri. Life as a child was hard, especially with untimely hard-ons in a class full of boys.

'Kneel down outside the class' shouts the Paadri. Sam follows Ray, and walks out of the class sullenly. All the students half-stand to see him kneel down outside the class room. Sam with his tool, popping northwards like a projectile from within his shorts, is sweating profusely.

Ray is red-faced.

Whispers of hushed gossip go around, as the most intelligent students, the prefect and his assistant, both Ray and Sam are reduced to being punished souls by Father Vargehese.

Father Varghese is also the teacher of moral science to the class. He shouts out at the two kids, 'Far from a perfect student, neither remaining a prefect, no chance of being the school head-boy anymore. Both of you. Pray that I do not rusticate you both. You Ray, should be expelled surely for this din in your class-room. '

There is a hushed silence in the entire class IX, section A, and the corridor outside. Prefects of all the other sections of grades IX and X walk till the doors of their classes. They all stare down the alley of eight classrooms at Sam and Ray. They both continue to kneel on their knees. A huge example is being made of the boys.

Ray is feeling like a flushed red rose plucked from its stem, thrown over a cactus of thorns on the floor, its petals strewn all over. In his remorse, he remains loyal as a friend could be, as he has refused to give a single name of the pesky students, especially Ray Lobo, Polly, or Happy, his playing mates.

As the classes break for the large recess, Sam is taken back in the class. As Father Varghese lectures Sam, Sam continues to say, 'yes Sir, yes Sir, Sorry sir...' for something that is really outside his adolescent control.

Ray has to continue to kneel down outside his class-room, the entire sections of classes pouring out of their rooms like water from a newly opened dam over the Mandovi, as the shrill school bell rings longer for the lunch recess.

Ray simply stares at the two ants on the tiled mosaic floor walking up the wall, and repeatedly falling down. It has now been three hours, yet he kneels fair and square, upright, with sweat on his brow, and his pencil thin moustache streaming salty water into his mouth. He is as famished with hunger as is Happy.

Happy, is left standing in his school shirt, covering his underpants, not a wee-bit ashamed or changed in attitude. He has been warned about being rusticated from school too by the Paadri, to no avail, giving no names of any student in the class.

Both Happy and Ray, bravely stick to their poses, till after recess, the deadline given to them by the tough Paadri. They have no time, to eat their meal, and notice that Polly has planned to leave them with no crumbs or biscuits from his own lunch box.

As the school bell continues to ring with a shrill tone, Roy Lobo passes by both of them in a jiffy, clutching his tiffin tightly, and disappears, running down the steps of the corridor to enjoy his lunch. He is eager to share the news with Polly and Sam.

Sam bellows at Lobo, even before Roy Lobo has opened his tiffin, 'Why did you not give Father Varghese the names of others to distract him away from Happy and Ray?'

'And make enemies forever? Happy and Ray are my friends forever. They can take this much of trouble for me, for my love for them.'

Polly smirks, agreeing with Lobo, 'A friend in need, is a friend indeed. Happy and Lobo know each other since kindergarten.'

'I have needs man. And Happy has always been kinder, while Ray is only keen to run in the garden, interested in his sports and prefect status. Serves them well.' laughs out Lobo and back slaps Polly.

Sam looks away in disgust first. He then looks at them, staring them down, picks up his own meagre canteen meal, and walks away from them toward a different corner in the cafeteria, leaving Polly and Lobo guffawing.

'He has no strain of *fun and masti* like us, with those two foolish buggers. He thinks he is a government by himself, let Sam go and lick their back-sides.' Lobo guffaws.

Sam mutters to himself, stuttering, while eating. 'What was that... only a pal in deeds, is a friend indeed? Ray has been let down, in need. Just that...only this, this...this does not bode well for our future together.'

Sam knows Ray well, coming as they do from the same lane of Betalbim's struggling fisherman colony.

The bonhomie did not remain the same in Goa's school that year. It was now bogus, and smelt of a put on bogey, a strong dislike for each other's values, and what each of them wanted to stand for.

Happy never knew how to hate anyone, so he would grace and say hello to Roy Lobo when they passed each other in school corridors.

Ray was not the kind to forget, and he felt it was up to the Paadri, or Jesus to forgive. Father Paadri played all kinds of tricks on Ray, called him over for confessions before each school teacher, first selectively, and then before the entire staff and teachers in the staff room.

This obsessive anxiety over Ray, to put him down made Father Varghese almost obsessively irritable and lose his own calm, and respect of the entire school. It was as if the entire sections of Grade IX and X now silently stood behind Ray, who came out stronger and spirited out of this power struggle.

A man with priestly responsibilities, teaching moral science to all the eight sections of Grade IX and X had come on too strong, appearing too tyrannical and eccentric. Boys who were back-benchers started throwing paper rockets, when his back was turned leaving the class-room.

Rather than showing empathy, Father Varghese looked to punish the children, for the smallest excuse, and often reprimanded even other bright children. The class environment became sombre and darker than usual, and students lost interest in moral science.

Religious discourse and punishments merged with each other, and God was projected as a higher power who could punish lower souls, especially naughty children.

Ray and Happy would run to pick up the paper planes, and the entire class would clap. Lobo would look on zealously, containing his sick aversion to friendship, and hide his fiendish behaviour, displaying a false calm and friendly disposition to Happy. Nothing changed between them.

Ray however had now started writing both their names on the black-board if they were to misbehave between classes, but never before Father Varghese' classes. The Paadri always got a clean black-board with no names, and the best behaved class before his period, not during it. The entire class was essentially supportive of Ray, to remain the prefect and be the head-boy of the school next year.

Yet, the Paadri chose Polly to be the head-boy next year, and even announced it in the school assembly before all grades of the Secondary school, awarding more than the requisite respect to the wealthy Polly. The position announcement a year before, would go to his inflated head and ego.

It allowed Ray to enjoy his time in school, study, play and participate in sports and other extra-curricular activities.

Ray had become the bugbear to Father Varghese and the *bete noire* to Roy Lobo.

Yet, he was the angel to Happy, and the soul mate to Sam. It was almost as if Ray was at once two different people.

5. Paronomasia

It is a form of a Pun, a kind figure of speech, where two words used, may sound the same but have different meaning

Illustration:

Forgive me my **Lord**. There is nothing in me to <u>laud</u>.
I hold the <u>cross</u>, yet, with me you must be <u>cross</u>.

5. Confession of a paadri

After the death of Ray, news reached the earlier school Paadri who was now the practicing priest at the Church of Mother Mary in Benoulim.

He was suddenly ridden with a serious sense of guilt for having seriously reprimanded his students over the years in school.

Very few of them had stayed back in the Goa of free India. Many had moved to nearby villages like Morpa, or closer to the Mahim church if they were fishermen, in Bombay. Those who wanted to pursue studies, were funded by wealthy Parsis using their relatives connections and moved to London. Some followed the Vasco coffin and the tales to Portugal.

The larger general public over the years stayed back to drink feni and work around the small medium or five star hotels based on their smarts. The more skillful and beach bums remained in the fishing profession, as the Arabian sea ran in their veins and arteries, like the high and low tides. A very select few tried to serve the needs of the Navy as it established its port around Vasco.

A select few came to church and even fewer made references of their school days, with any fondness toward Father Varghese.

Father Varghese usually heard the bickering of married couples as confessions. The wives complained why their sex lives were not better due to the fondness of coming home to drinks if not coming home drunk. The husbands complained their wives could not cook fish as good as their mummies, or even their wives mummies, and it led to bickering and bad taste both in marriage and the food table.

In this environment one day, Father Varghese made an attempt on a Sunday evening to make his own confessions to the Lord.

To an empty chair across his own chamber, he sat where many a young couple, old widow or drunken fishermen had sat before him to vent out their guilt. He had never betrayed anyone. Or Had he?

The Father decided to sit down and pray. A number of church-goer confessions ran through his grey cells. He tried to sift through them, to find his own true self.

He said a prayer, much to himself, as much to God.

Softly, Father Varghese spoke in the inner recesses of his mind, much about all his school days, his trainings before that, on how to become a priest. Images of Jesus on the cross flashed in his closed eyes. He clung hard for courage to the cross on his chest in the chain in his neck; he clung with the other hand the rosary beads he always held.

He smiled bemused over his musings when he was himself a young student at a Jesuit school in Kerala, so way back in time, that his eyes strained to think the period of time when he had really begun to believe in the story of Jesus. Somewhere he realized he just accepted the way of faith, and he could not remember his own folks, the face of his own father and mother were lost on him.

He only saw Mother Mary and the face of Jesus in his shut eyes.

Father Varghese spoke aloud his prayer. It was a soft voice from within that spoke, in a church devoid of people, only images, benches and the auditorium like hall, that had no echo.

It was his voice overflowing in words from his lips, coming from his heart, as each word fell on his chest with a thud. It relieved him of guilt, an expression of years of devotion, yet a confinement, of a holy life, but a rich realization of his own wrong, despite his sound counsel to so many who thought they were lesser souls.

Ψ

Prayer of a lifetime

Thank you my Lord, for a life
close to the divine

My soul could not become richer,
but I did not get poor either.

I wonder why I was dark and he was fair.
Jesus kept me safe.

Why there were always steps that led to an altar in the church?
Why the mass, so orderly always?

Why the men and women earlier sat separately?
Now together?

Why did Vasco really come to India?
Was it just the spices?

A thousand years later will he still be known as Vasco Da Gama or treated like some ancient European form of God, who descended to India?

I have so many thoughts oh God, to which I have no answers at my old age;
And I, myself have taught moral lessons to the children of a class.

I have reprimanded many sadly, for some reason or the other. Some severely. Some too severely and some because they were bad or ugly.

Father I can't take back my action, my deeds.
I must kneel down before you, and say sorry.
Especially to the soul of Ray.
Ray Noronha.

He was my best student.
I have done poorly to him many years back,

I hold the rosary beads, with the cross,
but you with me, must be cross.

I saw in his eyes, the mistake he made, he was scared and feared further reprimand of his friends.
So he took blame on himself.

I should have forgiven him.
Forgive me my Lord.
There is nothing in me to laud.

I am merely human.
I have erred.

Before you give me heaven or hell,

before you punish me, as I had punished him,
I must face my truth,
I was too severe, and stuck in false lie.

A lie, that punishment will make him good.
He was already too good for this world.
That is why you called him much before us.

I had rubbed his ears too hard, and confused him,
but not his soul.

As he knelt that day outside my class,
he begged for forgiveness for his friends,
...not for himself.

The sorry tears in his eyes, did not melt my heart of stone.
He ate nothing.

I was the Paadri, he was the scholar.
I made him kneel before me.

I had position and church behind me,
...he only had thee.

I kneel today My Lord, before you,
not for just forgiveness.
May my mistake cost me a harsh sentence,
Or punish me to your satisfaction.

In some way,
make me pay, as my guilt gets the better of me,
I cannot hear the confession of another,
as I cannot make my own to my own self any more

May **he be reborn**,
I pray to thee.

Let him take birth again,
with the same virtue, to protect his friends and brethren,
As he strived to do that day.

May he have the same soft eyes,
...and give him ability to forgive me, and his breatheren.
And me a chance to admit to him,
...that I wronged him and you in the same way.
With my harsh ways of punishment, over forgiveness.

To see you in him
and him with you,
is my only hope – with which I live.
Till I see him on the right side of heaven's heaven,
even if I am myself at the wrong side of hell's hell.

Ψ

Father Varghese completed his confession that night, but did not feel lighter. He wondered how many church-goers came to him admitting similar or worse. He also prayed deeply, that Ray is re-born. It was a blessing offered to heaven.

Paadri Varghese jumped from his terrace house, overlooking the steeple of the church at the stroke of daylight the next dawn.

It was reported in the Goa Times as a mystery, not clear, whether a Paadri committed suicide, or an ailing Father Varghese from the Church of Mother Mary, fell from his terrace house in the early hours of dawn.

Like many unsolved mysteries before the days of drugs and mafia, this one surrounding Father Varghese remained unsolved in the file of Goa Police Station at Benaulim.

PART – 2.

The *re-incarnation*

6. Anaphora – repetition

Is a figure of speech, with a deliberate repetition of a word or phrase at the begining of successive sentences.

Ilustration:

Life and death, life and death.

(Re-incarnation, re-birth is in most religious faiths, supported with consistency in their ideology – pure soul can never die, it can re-appear in another form or way of life force. More so, un-fulfilled souls.)

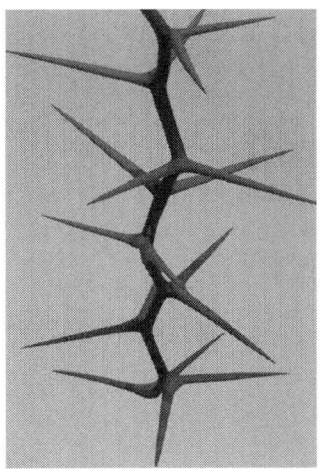

6. Picnic & Monkey Pranks

'**K**uber, sit tightly without moving. You have lice, and there is no other way to improve your hair *bacchey.*' Kuber's mother is on the verge of tears herself, as she tries to cajole him into being a statue. Her voice is laced with concern and trepidation.

Kuber was bawling, held tightly as he was between his fathers legs. The *Madaari* had his large sized pet monkey, gnaw with his nails and pull out the lice with his hands to enjoy his protein filled snack. Kuber's tears fell on the monkey's feet, as the primate winced with every tear falling on his feet claws, so did Kuber as the lice was pulled out. Kuber was petrified, and scared as he was, he did not muster the guts to look up.

'If you wish to go to Matheran for the school picnic, you better get yourself cleaned up and be prepared, there will be more monkeys there.' Kuber's father warned him.

The pampering mother interjects, before the father can further reprimand his son for having gotten his hair so filthy in the first place. 'Oh please let him be, and let this *Madaari* finish and leave first. I have already packed all his goodies into his school canvas bag.'

'The Scouts bag is also a waste, why did he not use that to pack his goods. He's a disgrace for having run away from the

Scouts outdoor plan, but is wiling to go galavanting with his school friends.'

Kuber with his head down, 'The entire Grade X of the school is going.'

'Are you prepared properly for your exams?' The father glares at Kuber's mother.

'Kuber, answer.' The mother finally looking at Kuber disapprovingly.

There is a muted silence. It remains that way over dinner, and Kuber slinks quietly into his bedroom in a hurry after his meal.

Next morning, the pampering mother still manages to get Kuber out of the house in time, to catch the school picnic bus.

Sid is already in the bus, sitting behind as he is, listening to the gloating Prahlad . 'I do not need the tutorials. I am already prepared for the prelims.'

Sid speaks flatly to his friend, not as his competitor but as his companion to assure him. 'I surely do. Need tutorials I mean.'

Prahlad feels reassured of his intelligence with the validation from Sid who is in the other B division of Grade X, while Prahlad thinks he is in Division A because he has all the intelligence of the world.

The rolly-polly Som Sarkaar chips in, 'After all Prahlad Ahuja is a master by himself, he has to stand first in the school boards this time.'

'Across Bombay Sarkaar, across Bombay, Prahlad has to come first.' Sid winks at Som.

An air of pomposity fills up in Prahlad as if he has swallowed the sea city air at the seashore, with the entire Arabian Sea in one gulp.

Both Som Sarkaar and Sid seated together, move to exchange their food packs and show-off to each other their list of rations. They work out an amicable way to share each other's food and decide to use the perishable products of both first, and save the cakes, biscuit packets and the Gujarati snacks that Sarkaar's mother has made at home for the last, when food at the lodge they are being accommodated at becomes unbearable.

They both have the same energy toward food, from their snacking outside the school compound gate for the street side peanut *'Chikki'*, to the rice based 'Idli' cakes in the school cafeteria. The picnic for them is about sports, playing T.T. and eating.

Kuber enters the bus with a scowl, and goes to the fag end of the bus to find Yug already seated there. With time, his mood improves, more so when Yug tells him there are Kitty Hawks available to prank over people. He confirms the rumours of classmates and information provided by Kuber's father, that there could be more than a few monkeys nearby the Lodge area, and to take precautions at night with his belongings.

Yug is the kid who is most conscientious at that age, but filled with mischief and an overall love for all the friends in the bus. He understands Prahlad, Kuber, Sarkaar and Sid in that order, while Sid alone gets along the best with Som and Yug equally himself.

It is Yug who is the bridge between the Kuber and Prahlad camp. This is because Sid and Sarkaar don't believe in camping or creating walls between friends.

History tells us, that the bond with Yug Prahlad and Kuber is strong as they consider themselves senior in their friendship, considering they are in the same school since inception of Kinder garden and are also area friends living in close proximity to each other. Yet, the three of them, incomplete in some way or the other, as a matter of traits, personality or kinship, easily accommodate Sarkaar and Sid who fill those same blanks, coming with their naturally affable nature, honest sincerity and love for food.

This binds the five of them into a kinship, that they refer to often, like the mythological brothers from different mothers, like the Pandavs of the historic Mahabharat lore.

Som has often cautioned each of them, warning them of the side effects of the Mahabharat, including the sharing of one wife, which would be impossible between them and for the times they live in, to which each friend often jibes the other about the kind of wife he will get and will be more suited to.

Yug and Sid do not attempt to conform or like all this even for the sake of group dynamics and offer no lip service or humouring their sense of what comprises a joke. It earns them the title of Arjun and Bhim.

Sid is cynical and real at the same time. All he has to say is, '*Jay Bhim*' in return, referring more to the adage used by his 'gully' friends who like him are all followers of Dr. Ambedkar. He also conforms if anything else, to his appetite and sense of looking for justice, with that slogan.

'Don't teach us the constitution of India, we have full knowledge of it's place in civics and history.' proclaims Prahlad , feeling challenged again.

Sarkaar whispers in Sid's ears 'He is constitutionally correct, but ignorant, that Bhimrao was Dr. Ambedkar's given name.' Sid nods in silence with a smile.

Yug uses this banter always, including in the bus, 'None of you can be married, till I hit the eye of the fish and win our wife in the Swayamwar. These other two are not so important as no one remembers their role in the war.'

It is the only time, they can collectively shut Prahlad up, so even Kuber joins in the laughter and acknowledges the camaraderie that Yug manages to stitch up.

They like to rib tickle each other, and often pick up the bag, like in their class, of their weak classmate Lokesh, and throw his bag around all over the bus.

Till the bag reaches Sid, who inspects it, finds food in it, and decides to return it back to Lokesh. The weak boy is profusely thankful to Sid, to have provided a sense of justice and fairness in the bus.

All the class mates fear Sid for his known clout with all the teachers travelling on the picnic, and no one wants scout or watch duty at night, so they back off.

Yug pulls Kuber back and hisses him into silence.

The bully in Kuber feels that a missed opportunity can provide a chance for revenge later that night, and whispers a plan in Yug's ears, who only shakes his head with laughter.

He tells Kuber to keep his plan to himself, signalling 'finger on your lips.' in a mime.

Sid on the other hand, has often picked up Som Sarkaar from his house on his bicycle and ridden both together to the school. They both have joined the secondary school in later years, and inched themselves up in sight of the other three, due to their academic excellence. It is with Prahlad's recognition of their merit in some subjects, yet not all that their bonhomie clicks.

While Sarkaar naturally likes Biology, Sid has been fond of Algebra and Physics. The former keen to become a doctor while Sid being an Architect's son is keen to be one.

Yug comes from the family background of money lenders; yet is not the most shrewd of them all.

Kuber and Prahlad, are sons of builders, yet do not share that much of a bond, as Kuber has been always jealous of the rich family wealth that Prahlad seems to gloat over; 'Material is immaterial' remains Prahlad's philosophy, after he is done self proclaiming and misusing his intelligence as a badge of higher status.

The bus is on its way to Karjat in half an hour.

The child in each kid is ecstatic just knowing about a toy train journey that follows the bus ride, with a plan to descend toward the railway station of Neral to go onward to Matheran on the single gauge line.

The kids are all excited as they are yet on the verge to go from boys to men. Some of them giggle as they can be mistaken for young girls, while others have thin broomstick facial air, that would make a cat's whiskers in comparison, look like hairy dogs ears.

Ψ

Monkey Pranks

A hundred fifty of the boys disembark form the bus, and after the count of the P.T. sir and blowing of his whistle, the train engine responds with a loud whistle over it.

The train chugs slowly upward toward its destination. Each window facing kid has his elbow parked outside the window grills, some trying to feel the brisk air with their fingers. Many are digging into their lunchboxes, eating excessively and before time.

At Neral station, the kids again disembark with their canvas bags, flying out of the train like bees from a hive. The students had been briefed by the school teachers on the toy train, that they would have to walk till the lodge, a mini trek of sorts.

Some of the older teachers, join their coach accompanied by a stocky tall lad called Dinshaw, who leads them with horses toward Dasturi Naka – the gate before main Matheran.

Yug and Kuber walk kicking the red sand at their friends ahead, with Prahlad taking the brunt of it. Sarkaar is mesmerized with the number of horses, while Sid clings on to his bag, knowing that the swinging monkeys from trees and rooftops above, could cost them their weekend ration of yummy treats.

Prahlad was at the pulpit of his mind's chapel. As they enter the lodge premises, his grave concern doubles. He feels he is too important to share a bunk bed with anyone. As it is, it is his first time in quarters that he finds to be very sub-standard compared to the luxury of his home, where he alone shares the master bedroom of the adjoining apartment to his parents, with just himself.

Here he was to share company with Yug, who he instructed to climb to the upper section of the bunk bed. The real reason being the fear Prahlad had of falling off the bed when in deep slumber, as he was accustomed to falling on his soft Persian rug below his bed at home. There used to be pillows to soften his fall, which were missing what with just one flour shaped concoction, *'That must be a two hundred year old jute, rather than cotton cushion used by one of the Jai Bhims,'* he spoke aloud to himself.

Yug pitying him adjusted as always, and threw his stuff at the top deck, and ran out to look for Kuber.

As they were awarded their rooms based on their class sections and divisions, Kuber was thrown in the company of Sarkaar and Sid. It was Kuber and Yug's plan to scare Sarkaar and Sid at night, which now became a three way plan shared with Prahlad, on Yug's insistence.

After dinner, the three of them gang up. Kuber play acts that he will turn and go to sleep, while Sid actually fell asleep.

Once Sarkaar is in the common toilet for his customary beauty bath before bed-time, and Sid was in deep sleep, Kuber tip-toes to open the section of his Lodge, to allow Prahlad and Yug the access to enter in. All three of them take positions outside Sarkaar's bathroom, wearing their monkey caps in reverse.

As they hear Sarkaar turn the noisy tap to a close position, the water stops falling into the steel bucket, creating what their History teacher Mrs. Samant would call, *'Peen drop silenns pleees' they speak in a whisper of muffled unison through the wool over their eyes and mouth.*

As Sarkaar opens the door of his bathroom, they jump him with a shout, to which Sarkaar dropping his towel, runs back into the toilet naked shouting, *'Mummyeeeee!!!'*

It is a shrill scream that echoes inside the lodge, but does not awaken Sid back in his bunker room.

The gang of three, tip-toes out of the lodge, after bolting Sarkaar's door from the outside. Kuber, the last who stood watching him skid into the bathroom on the slippery floor, can see him fall on his rotund buttocks and bum-skate to the end of the floor; and knock his head on the wall of the other end,

Kuber picks up the towel, and throws it outside the lodge behind the bushes as he exits.

Prahlad and Yug, are happy to have pulled off a plan, and host Kuber late into the night in their room, chomping on the masala peanuts robbed from Sid's bag.

The devious pleasure of Kuber is complete, as he has locked them both from the outside, leaving Sid with no option to visit the bathroom, and Sarkaar to leave it.

Som Sarkaar has no option to wear any clothes, devoid even of the towel, shivering naked into the night.

Chaos prevails next morning, as Sarkaar and Sid miss their head count at breakfast and an assembly is called by their teacher, *'Rudy Sir.'* The proud P.Ed teacher, Rudy, is accompanied by his friend Maneckji's son, Dinshaw, who prides himself on his role model Rudy Sir, for his fitness, hockey dribbling and the moustache that Rudy Sir sports.

Dinshaw is called *'young man'* by Rudy sir who always pulls at Dinshaw's minuscule whiskers, that he has retained to impress his role model.

Rudy sir can always do with some junior help, what with these tiny tots as scouts he leads at St. Patricks. Dinshaw is built differently, like a greek athlete who can swim, play hockey and throw down the biggest wrestling competitor from St. Patrick's down to the ground with a one arm manoeuvre.

'A moustache is one that grows on it's own, without shaving, my young man, unlike the greens that all your little daisy friends sport by visiting the barber repeatedly. I hope they are not missing in the loins department unlike you. I'm sure you carry a large hammer under your shorts unlike their small spanners!'

Dinshaw enjoys the adult status, over the fledglings from St. Patrick's and the respect of his manhood, of which he does not get much at home.

While Maneckji as the Physics teacher is absent in Matheran; *he much prefers Panchgani and Mahabaleshwar for his camps;* Dinshaw is overjoyed for being sent as the junior Maneckji.

For ever and ever during his school holidays on Saturdays, Dinshaw has been in awe of Rudy Sir. That includes his coaching and his style of hosting the entire sports day at the St. Patrick's School.

Dinshaw was enrolled by his parents in the much acclaimed RSS boarding school at Mahabaleshwar, and is here looking for a physical challenge in this holiday cum camp of 10th graders. He is their senior by two years and is zealously keen to fill in his father's large shoes, which he cannot at home or at St. Patricks School.

'My son shall not study, where I teach,' being Adil Maneckji's maxim, as he wants Dinshaw to learn *'in a different environment from these convent school sanitized ponds.'*

It is Dinshaw's dream, to be the P.T. teacher assistant to Rudy Sir at St. Patricks; testing all the teachers fitness for a run and discuss throw. He imagines his father coming last in that race, and dropping the discuss throw on his own foot, and a javelin throw of another teacher stabbing his father Adil in the butt.

His dream comes to an end, as Rudy Sir commences a search for Sarkaar and Sid, sending out horses toward the station road, and marshals all the house captains to be led by Dinshaw for a search of all the lodges.

Rudy sir bellows, 'I will check all the rooms, and any mischief reported by a student of our own school that has caused Sarkaar or Sid to go missing, will lead to you missing your prelim exams, and me asking for your rustication. Come forward and own up.'

As Yug is about to step out of line to claim he has information, Kuber steps on his feet. Prahlad develops an anxiety that he has never felt in his examinations and breaks into a dozen non-stop hiccups. Rudy sir comes up close to his face on his walking drill, and freezes in front of him and Kuber

They look into each other's eyeballs, as Rudy sir can only see himself in their dark eyes.

In the meanwhile, Dinshaw goes running from room to room, till he discovers Sid knocking on his own room door. He unlocks the door, and out comes Sid gushing, ' I have been knocking since two hours in the morning, where are Kuber and Sarkaar?'

An Ayah, comes out of the section of doors leading to the common bathroom and toilets of the lodge, wailing, 'A boy is lying splattered on the floor, facing the wall of the bathroom sir. He is naked and seems to have fainted, but luckily there is no blood.'

'That is worse, there could be internal bleeding.'claims Rudy Sir.

All the house captains followed by Dinshaw and Rudy Sir run up the steps. As they find him, they collect together in a huddle to comfort and robe Sarkaar while Sid hovers behind them to ensure his pal's safekeeping. They take Som Sarkaar to Sid's room.

The school assembly of students breaks up and the gang of three get into a huddle behind a banyan tree.

'We should own up. Sarkaar will spill the beans to Rudy Sir.' Prahlad is the first to lose his cool.

Kuber in full confidence mode, 'Nothing like this will happen, Sarkaar is too embarrassed and scared himself to reveal anything. The whole school would have seen his polly and rotund bum now, and he will take time to recover himself.'

Yug is silent in a daze. He has participated in a prank, that he never expected to have gone so wrong, and he has to comfort his conscience into silence. The heaviness of his guilt is weighing him down and he can feel the redness climb from the back of his ears, as he develops a headache.

Prahlad is close to bawling, when Kuber runs away with another set of friends from his 'Green house' at the pretext of calling the teachers who led the team of horses toward the station to get them back to the base of the Lodge.

Yug speaks in a morose low tone, as any school going kid who has failed his exams and is standing before his parent with the report card, 'We are as good as the company we keep.' He looks toward Prahlad, who is still panicking about his being removed from school and thereby his chance of coming first in the school and the entire city of Bombay being compromised.

Prahlad's self talk and mumbo-jumbo is lost in the din of Dinshaw using a loud speaker to shout out aloud that '*Sarkaar and Sid have been found.*'

Loud whistles are being blown on all four sides of the Lodge as a pre-set signal to let all the classes know. A roar of '*hip hip hurray*' ricochets all around the British built lodge, and the boys playing volleyball, start kicking it around for sheer pleasure. The two boys found were heroes till then, now they are super-heroes.

Sid walks up to Yug near the football goal post, 'You are as good a friend, as your deed Yug. You will hopefully remember this for the rest of your life.' Sid's tone is that of reprimand.

Yug and Prahlad spin around to see Sid standing before them.

'Why this animosity, this cruel competitive charade of friendship? What you want and regale in, is just pure silly meanness.' Sid waits silently for a repartee that usually comes from Prahlad, the head, and not Yug the body of the monster they are now together. He looks around for the heart and spirit, Kuber, who may be cheaply mourning his lost victory.

Yug looks up at Sid, his entire face going red. The admittance of guilt on his face writ large. It is enough for Sid to understand the real master-mind behind the prank, who is missing from the scene of crime.

Sid threatens, 'Tell Kuber, I will get him. If he does not sleep in our room, it will be known to the entire school tonight, who was behind this juvenile prank.'

Ψ

Dinshaw is not far behind, so Sid walks away in a huff, leaving Prahlad and Yug to pantomime as if they are looking for lost marbles.

Prahlad removes some new marbles from his back-pocket and begins to crouch for an aim toward a squirrels hole in the bark of the tree. Yug cannot get up from his posture with his back bent and leaning on the tree.

'Any clue who was behind all this? I thought you all were pretty thick, as I had an eye on you during the bus and train ride here. Rudy Sir is pretty upset. A punishment is due to someone,' exclaims Dinshaw.

Prahlad manages to hit the first marble he had thrown, with the second one while standing, his two legs spread wide. 'How would we know? Our rooms are on the floor above in the next annexe of the Lodge building where Sarkaar was bathing.'

'You do know the place Sarkaar was bathing!' comes out Dinshaw.

Yug turns a crimson red in his face.

Dinshaw turns back to the lodges where he came from, to look for Rudy Sir.

Prahlad goes back to playing with his marbles, while Yug tries to regain a normal hue of skin tone, and his poise back. The two spend their lunch cursing Kuber, and looking out for him till late after dinner.

At ten that same night after the dining hall shuts down for all meals, and his milk and custard is over, Kuber enters the room to sleep, filled to his heart's content with the days pranks, meals and mischievousness that he calls healthy fun. He ignores Sid who is dressing a twisted ankle of Sarkaar, seated at his feet.

A tear drops out of Som Sarkaar's blazing angry eyes, yet Kuber nonchalantly swings from the head-board side of the bunk bed, rattles it to shake up the entire bed post, and jumps onto his mattress, causing the creaking of the wood boards below in the room.

Sarkaar has had both his meals in the room, not being able to face the rest of the school friends, nor finds any pleasure in the meal activity that day. He has developed a low grade fever, and his nose drips, otherwise his heavy buttocks feel warm again with two warm blankets, one tucked above and another under him. It is only his bandaged ankle and one side of his hip that aches.

'The entire room stinks of balm.' The voice comes from over their heads.

Sid stands up and stares hard at Kuber, who flatly replies with a 'Whaaat?? Did you guys think you are Gandhi and Ambedkar?'

'I do realize today, you three are surely Gandhi's monkeys.'

Sid's terse comment shuts up Kuber, who turns over to sleep but faces the wall and stares at it with his large beady eyes.

Sarkaar is unable to say anything; he too turns over his unbruised hip, and goes to sleep.

Ψ

7. Simile

A figure of speech, where two similar things are directly compared to be alike.

Illustration:

'turtle...its like a tortoise, no, it's a turtle.'

7. A Monkey in bed.

At sunrise around 7am, there is a scratching sound at the footboard side of the bunk-bed.

A bleary eyed Kuber shakes his head in disbelief. He tries to scream and shriek out of bed, and nearly falls over. He looks below to find two monkeys in the room sitting atop Sarkaar and Sid's empty bags, with contents spilt all over.

Trembling atop in an Indian toilet pose over his pillow, Kuber begins to howl meekly, *'Save me, save me.'*

The monkey crouched on his blanket at his foot-stand of the bunk-bed, first reaches out with his hand and offers him a banana from a large stalk of over two dozen bananas.

Upon watching Kuber with uncertainty, it first scowls back, and then shrieks and screams back, showcasing it's bright white teeth, compared to the furry brown all over it's body.

It's two primate friends at the bottom of the bed, also scream and scowl back each time Kuber attempts to howl.

Kuber's eyes are filled with fear, all his hair standing on end. There are banana peels all over the room, and there are over a dozen un-eaten bananas spread all over Kuber's bed.

As he howls and places his hands over his face and eyes, Kuber simultaneously feels a cold yet burning sensation on his back and in his eye-lids. He can smell the *Binaca toothpaste* he had used last night, and slowly leaks urine into his own pyjamas. He cannot hold back, as he is overcome with fear.

In the other room, Prahlad and Yug awaken to havoc caused by a single large female monkey. The *brown bandar* has chubby cheeks, and chunkier breasts. It is blowing kisses to them from below as they both cling to each other on the bunk bed above.

A small baby monkey that had gone unnoticed, climbs up and down the ladder of the bunk bed in a circular gamesmanship which neither Yug nor Prahlad reciprocate.

'The mummy monkey wants you to play with her son.' Sid is standing at the door of the room, with a laughing Sarkaar on his side.

'Please rescue us Sid! We will be indebted to you forever. It was Kuber's idea.' Prahlad pleads. Yug nods an affirmation.

'We know.' replies Sarkaar, 'This is ours.'

Sid lets out a wry smile. 'Hold your pee, your monkey in the other room could not. He has wet his bed, so we are looking out for another room. We got you this mother son pair to make plans for other pranks of the day.'

Now the mother monkey also nods. It appears to be too satiated or old to move. The younger nimble monkey is going ballistic on it's joy ride up and down the ladder of the bunk bed.

'We won't, we won't!' exclaims Yug.

Sid responds, 'Gandhiji would be sad to see his three monkeys this way. You three did not do anything?'

Sarkaar chips in, 'After all you never saw anything, you never said anything, and you never heard anything.'

Both of them leave the door open, throwing a hefty banana stalk filled with over two dozen of the fruit into the deep end of the room near the bed.

As they walk away, Sarkaar taunts them, 'Enjoy the breakfast. It may just be your lunch and dinner too.'

As they walk down the steps, each of them give a hand-clap to Dinshaw standing outside the tail end of the corridor. 'Rudy Sir has sent all your school mates to the town centre, no one returns till five. These are trained primates from the village, they will do no harm, other than scowl and smile.'

Sarkaar is laughing as he looks toward Sid, 'Thanks my friend, I hope the monkeys step out before the two of them shit in bed too.'

'Mention not buddy. I hope the monkeys don't stay indoor and imitate them and shit there too.' Sid looks ahead happy that a sense of justice has prevailed, albeit with some Scouts boys help, 'Din-Din and I go a fair way back. Not many know, I have played hockey and cricket with him in the park around our school.'

Dinshaw following them, has Sid's back, 'They had all gone bananas. Serves them right, we just got them the right breakfast.'

'And their own company.' Sarkaar looks backwards beyond Dinshaw and says a '*thank you*' quietly in his mouth.

Dinshaw just salutes back like a scout. He places his three open fingers on his right forehead toward Sarkaar.

Sid turns back and salutes Dinshaw, 'The thumb over the index finger, is a mark for the *strong to protect the weak*. You my friend have made a friend for life. You are a friend in deed.'

Dinshaw responds in a duty posture, his salute continuing now to himself. His chest filled with pride that he could come of use to Rudy Sir. 'Indeed. Duty toward others, and toward religion or country. These primates are better than your so-called pals. They are more trustworthy and loyal. Your school mates break the basic tenets of **Scouts** Law of being **friendly courteous and kind**!'

'It goes back to 1900's.' for a minute, Sid becomes quiet, pensive and then sullen.

Sarkaar now fills in the silence left by a now silent Sid, 'Nor are they obedient, thrifty or brave. They are cheerful one instant and manipulative another.'

'It is not just Kuber Savla?' asks Dinshaw.

Sarkaar responds to Dinshaw, 'Prahlad is carried away by Kuber and Yug is just happy to imitate Prahlad for opinion. He validates everything that Prahlad says or does.'

'Our Matheran monkey friends are better.' As the words are out of Sid's mouth, he gets a sense of deja-vu, as if he knew all these events will take place.

'Or has this taken place before?' he says much to himself. He meanders into the grassy part of the path from the Lodge, closes his eyes to see flashes of images in his mind. They are of an island, of the waves of an ocean, monkeys running across a sand bar of land.

Dinshaw and Sarkaar have walked ahead. Sid falls onto his knees, and can hear some faint music in the background. It appears to be a very different tune, one he has never heard before. It goes, 'Ghe ghe ghe ghey re, ghe re sahiba....' and then a lilting tune set to...'ma ya yaya ya, ma ya yaya ya....'

'Where's Sid?' Dinshaw looks up at Sarkaar.
'What's happened to him now?' says Sarkaar turning back.

Sid is looking upward toward the sky,... 'a tur...turtle...its like a tortoise, no, it's a turtle. It has begun swimming,...it has stopped,...it is looking at me in the face. I can see a young boy, bleeding from one eye, face in the sand...'

Dinshaw runs back to find his friend in the grass, paralyzed. He stands behind Sid, afraid that he may completely collapse. Aghast, Sarkaar is astonished too, 'With whom is he talking?'

Sid speaks as if in someone else's voice, 'The shell of a turtle is my safe heaven, a secure place, one for the spirit. The soul finds peace and safety in it's refuge. A sense of tranquility.' Sid faints with sudden exhaustion, holding his one hand atop his head.

He is caught by Dinshaw, as he is about to fall face down in the soil, where the class mates were playing volleyball the previous morning.

Sarkaar says, 'We should not play with mother nature, but from monkeys, to turtles??? That is a bit unexpected at this height. I have seen him earlier in school too, it is seldom that Sid gets these migraine headaches.'

'It could be low sugar or salt. Perhaps it's just his blood pressure gone haywire. Unless it is some disturbing memory from another incident, perhaps a visit to the zoo?'

Dinshaw lifts his friend in one swift action, and hauls him over his shoulders, as a coolie would with a bed mattress at the Railway station of Matheran.

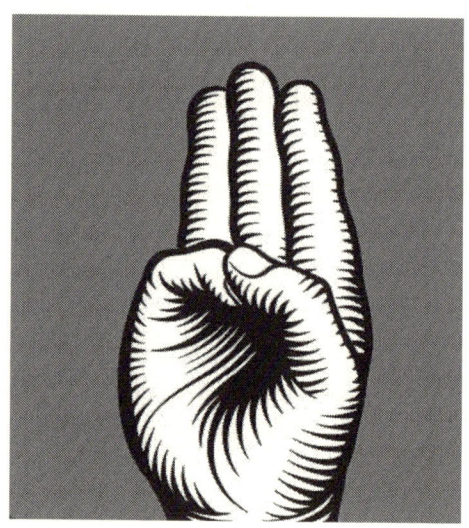

8. Litotes

A figure of speech that uses a Double negative. An exaggerated language to opposite effect.

Illustration:

'He is not that bad. He is not your enemy.'

8. Self interest in College

Can you ever befriend the enemy?
But what do you do with a friend, who does not get better?

If you can make him bitter, you sure can make a bigger enemy of him.

All you can do, is not judge him, wrongly.

'The best fortress is to be found in the love of the people. For all though you may have a fortress, they will never save you if you are hated by the people.' Machiavellian's cynical view of humans is that people are fundamentally self-interested. This will play out in their relationships.

That is what happened to Kuber.

Over the years all five of them land up in the Architecture discipline.

Sarkaar finishes his Grade XII in disappointment and fails to score in the Biology department, despite what he thinks are good lab practicals and written examinations. Sarkaar has to face the displeasure of leaving his cosy home, his diabetic mother and the peer group he has grown up with to catch the train to Sholapur with his father. Mr. Ravi Sarkaar Kapadia is waiting at the foot board of the station as Sarkaar dials the house phone of Sid, 'I am leaving for Sholapur my friend. I do not think I had the luck to be with you.'

'Do not blame luck, it is our destiny that you too will be an Architect like each one of us. Who had thought in school days we will come so far?'

'Yet, *only I will be quite far* now...'

'You are in Maharashtra, catch a train and come back in the holidays, how far is Bombay? We will paint the town red and eat in all the Udipi joints once you are back.'

'Hurry up Sarkaar, the train is about to leave.' shouts Mr. Kapadia.

'Go my friend, go with a smile, you are lucky your father is accompanying to drop you, my dad is in office and does not know what field I will enrol in today afternoon.'

Sid finds out later that noon, that he is not the only one to have been short-listed. Many are higher on the same list due to their surnames and quota for the community, as the private Architecture college has been set up by the benevolent Mr. Batumal Modani, an immigrant to Bombay due to India's partition.

The other three have done reasonably well, and one of them reunite with him. Yug is ahead in the admissions queue at the Batumal trust run Architecture college. The mini-campus is at the heart of their Bombay city; Bandra suburb is still empty during the day despite the bustling commercial street of Linking Road.

Sarkaar's arch nemesis Kuber, soon descends from an auto-rickshaw, and runs into the admission queue, joining at a point ahead with Yug. Some students in line object and try to push Kuber aside, who ignores their pleas and gets in like a fat rat into a small hole left by an unhurried student, now behind him.

Kuber's mindset matches that of auto-rickshaw drivers of the city, who will swerve and bend into any crevice and corner left on the streets, to get two inches ahead of a slowing down car or taxi.

Sid who has secured 96% marks in the board exams is left behind by over thirty spots in the line of meritocratic students, who await their confirmation of the preferred courses they have selected – Drawing & Design, Architecture or Civic & City Planning – something that is most sought after due to the brain drain from India to America of the 1990's.

Any Architect staying back in India is lapped up for jobs by international companies entering India, if the students do not leave for the U.K. or U.S. of A; the preferred location for Architects to migrate to.

It is as if the late Batumal Modani has opened up the course in Bombay only for immigration of his community of people out of India.

As the rush piles up, the tight campus in the fledgling five story building, resembles a line outside the ticket window of a first class railways pass at Bandra station. The meritocratic have to develop patience to be in line everywhere, unlike those with their connects and networks or community card, sometimes even the backward caste.

Yug and Kuber secure their admissions in their preferred courses of Design and Architecture within the first hour. To feel superior is a matter of community pride for them, especially when they were laggard nerds in the making during school days. This gives them a new sense of bonding with each other and one-upmanship over Sid. It is a matter of being communal rather than congenial within the community.

Standing in that line, Sid too realizes the challenge he must face in the years ahead, knowing that Sarkaar has not made it for admissions in Bombay. Sid is also aware, that the really other intelligent student from his school - Prahlad, has shown himself as a Backward community with a paid fudged certificate, to get admitted in the government grant college of Queen Victoria's School of Architecture.

'After all, merit is immaterial?!' says Sid to himself. He remains quiet, sullen yet confident and retains his position in line.

'Thinks of himself as today's Gandhi...' sneers Kuber as he passes by Sid, talking as if to the boy behind him. Yug stops by to greet and meet with Sid, to join him and tell him the seats balance that are still vacant for the rest of them in line.

Yug instills some confidence in Sid, 'You will perhaps get the admit in Civic & City Planning, the least preferred course as of now, but take it. We will be together in the first year classes, and you will surely do better than most of us who have a concession certificate due to the communal preference of our community. You can always switch into your preferred field next year. They are taking note of your preference when you take the admit in Civic Planning.'

As Sid's turn comes up closer, there is a document verification line, which checks the domicile of the students. Father's name. Sid is asked. 'Mr. Sunil Bhandari,' he replies. As soon as he takes his name, his father bursts on the scene, entering the gate of the building and waving from afar. Sid breaks into his trademark wry smile. As Mr. Bhandari approaches the payment counter where Sid is the immediate person in line, he acknowledges and thanks Yug, assuming that he has been keeping him company.

'Sorry son, there was no transport from Bandra station and it took time from Churchgate to reach here, as I had to walk hurriedly. I am carrying the money needed for the fees.'

Sid looks toward Yug, 'Whatever happens, happens for the best. You carry on with Kuber, I will be going home.'

As the payment receipt is issued to Mr. Bhandari, they both walk away overjoyed, that Sid has secured admission in a nearby college as he is now less than half an hour from home. Sid thinks of the morning conversation with Sarkaar, and in his mind thanks his stars that his father made it on time.

In the nick of time.

He stares at the Maharashtra state examination board xeroxed papers, and looks at the square red box saying 'ADMIT' back at him in uppercase lettering. He wished, that the unscrupulous school mates would *admit*, that they erred in their judgement on him and Sarkaar. Perhaps it was too late too wait for the acceptance of his friends who never walked the tight rope of idealism like him.

Prahlad had joined the government college the previous day and any sense of balance he could expect, would be missing now.

Sid thought, 'I may as well concentrate what I am good at, - and that is academic studies. Let's wait and watch and leave the tom foolery to them.'

9. Apostrophe

A Figure of speech that is a direct address to the dead or the absent. This is a special form of personification.

Illustration:
'Oh Yug, Oh Prahlad come!'

9. Time Pass.
Time, passes.

As months pass, they find themselves in the second year.

Kuber has found himself a girlfriend from a simple Rajasthani family. The word spreads all over the college that she apparently finds him extremely charming and charismatic, something that the manipulative Kuber has himself spread to his class and juniors.

He showcases her and respects her intelligence on the face of things, but squarely likes it that, 'I am the one gaining in popularity – finally! That too before our graduation is complete.'

Yug finds it extremely difficult to make any commitment toward anyone in particular and is streamed into the same classes with Sid, who keeps himself in high spirits in female company. They occasionally saunter into drawing projects and project case study experiments together. They choose the comfort of a known past bonhomie, rather than an unknown devil.

Sid continues out of his helpful nature to help Yug understand structural drawings and interpretations. They explore the study of international architecture though they make lofty goals of staying back in India.

Kuber gets busy with Rekha, Yug clings to Sid for familiarity and knowledge, while Sid enjoys to eat his meals now with Yug post campus studies. They often make cyclostyling trips together to the nearby Bandra station shops that loudly claim '*XEROX*' for the lack of the same brand's machines inside their premises.

At one fourth a rupee per page, Sid gets entire textbooks cyclostyled and bound together for himself and Yug, by riding his scooter up and down, quickly eating a lunch together on the move or while waiting outside the Xerox shops and coming back in time to return the reference books to the library.

In the course of the final semester of the second year, both Yug and Sid become inseparable as they push the pedal hard via reference and joint study programs. They goad each other to achieve results higher than they both expect and claim that, 'We are nearly 1/2 an Architect now' to each other, by increasing the sheer hours of hard work.

They try to understand as much as logic behind their subjects though they both know, that seldom will it come all in use in practical day to day life.

At the time of results, Rekha is exasperated and tensed as she knows she will not do very well, much of her time having gone in galavanting with Kuber.

Kuber seems to have his well oiled machinery at work with the teaching assistants and administrative staff, to look out for him. They share his set paper questions and he prepares himself just enough to scrape through, or use his influence to get higher than his score when required by greasing the palms of the back-end administrative staff.

He often walks in and out of the registrar's office, and seems to know his way around the place as if he is a working employee.

After the conclusion of examinations it is judgement day. Rekha passes out before the board listing of exam results for A.T.K.T.'s (Applied to keep terms) as she ducks in three out of her six papers. There is a crowd of students around the board who help to seat her and comfort her for future course of action. Rekha is the only batch mate who will have to repeat the year, or carry these papers into the next year and clear them along with the third year courses, a gigantic task of nine papers.

That evening Kuber lands up at Yug's house, requesting him to become an accomplice to fix her marks in one of the papers that he feels she will find impossible to clear even on her second attempt.

Yug out of sheer curiosity joins Kuber after dinner to visit the college administrative staff, where Kuber has greased the palms of someone to convert Rekha's score of 30, to look like an 80 in the system. Kuber hand writes the answers copied from Rekha's class mate, after sitting for an hour in the college administration office of the college.

The peon, and the administrative assistant have promised Kuber ninety minutes of time to fill in her unused sheets, change the scores, add marks with a red pen for the scores to add up, while Yug is waiting down pacing silently for Kuber.

Yug is hoping he and Kuber get out of the college building unseen by the resident principal who sleeps and resides on campus accommodation next door. It is known that Mr. Manoj Kumar, is no less patriotic than the hero of the same name, and that he would do his nightly rounds at the back of the campus post dinner.

Kuber races out unseen, and hides on the first floor landing steps as the principal is taking the vertical elevator downstairs. He lets Principal Manoj Kumar turn toward the gardens when he signals to Yug to move out of the college compound by using the back common entrance with NNK Commerce college so that the principal mistakes him for another student, if he is sighted at all.

Circling directly and cooly walking behind Manoj Kumar himself, Kuber walks out of the college gate on the left, when the principal turns right wards to continue his walks on campus. He pushes the Fiat car of his father in neutral, and lets Yug join him to push the car down the lane.

After about two hundred meters both sit in the car quietly, and Kuber nods with his impish expression gesturing away Yug's worried look.

'It took a while longer than expected, I had promised Dad I was going down to buy a Paan, so let's pick that up from *Paagal Paan Bhandar* and head back.' Kuber pushes the car into third gear without really checking with Yug.

Yug reprimands, 'You really the mad *paagal* guy! Chew some sense into your head rather than chewing on betel leaves.'

Kuber suggestively speaking, 'You spend too much time with that staid Sid my boy. What's the fun in life without some risks? It will solve Rekha's problems otherwise she will end up repeating a year. All of you are a bit too serious and over committed in the Architect and Drawing design courses. It is the Architecture that is Architecting all of you guys. There are other things to do, including visiting the newly opened amusement park Esselworld.'

'Yeah, why bother to study aspects of subjects that she will never use ever again, other than to write exams,' agrees Yug, always willing to be led into a different kind of thinking. 'I am happy to visit Esselworld.' Yug is always willing to see new places, as he tries to see the other's point of view.

'At this rate, we can wrap up our courses in four years and spend a year of fun, before each of us flies out of India. I believe that the five year degree is just a piece of paper that will help us to get out of the country,' Kuber speaks with an intention to tempt and distract.

'Kuber, I do not think my family will have the resources. And Sid also does not intend leaving the country, or the city for that matter,' clarifies a humble Yug.

Kuber again steers the conversation away, 'Look up to Prahlad my friend. Sid sets the moral bar too high, and is a bit too idealistic for today's times.'

Yug speaks his heart finally, 'Well so does Prahlad. I am not so resourceful, nor can I compete with both of them. I have to see what suits my family.' Yug is more realistic and wishes to live within his limits. 'Anyways, Pomposity thy name is Prahlad; it is just that I cannot bring myself to tell him that. He is my friend, not my role model,' Yug explains himself.

'Yes, Prahlad is too proud, and filled with vanity my friend, that is a bad mix.' Kuber seems to be driving around longer than what was intended initially. He wants to try and control the narrative and manipulate the closeness that Yug feels with Prahlad, toward himself. 'Go on, feel free to express yourself,' says Kuber, to get Yug to think like himself.

'Well, in the other corner is your favourite Sid. He suffers from neither, except making us suffer his humility all the time. Maybe he will soon be sitting with Shroff to teach the juniors next.' Yug and Kuber both laugh at that jointly.

Yug self realizes, thinking to himself, that he is just going along with what Kuber is saying, though he has never himself seriously thought about these things, till they have been brought up. He does not enjoy this gossip and rumour mongering, yet he partakes in it without any guilt or remorse. He has said, only what Kuber wants to hear.

'I do concede, he is able to look at a page of paper in any book, memorize while grasping it, even remember the page number, the drawings, and place in the text books that a particular subject matter appears. I can rarely surpass him in grit or concentration, and he does not gloat or care about his intellect. He uses it only to give the examinations and takes a solid break between semesters.' Kuber admits to his favouritism, concluding, 'He remains the best human being, mercurial at times if he has to reprimand wrong doing, but helpful always. It is a boon to have him in our college with us, I recognize that. It makes him my benchmarking favourite. Just that he rarely meets us at Prahlad's house to play board games or...'

Yug, finally fed up of this obsession with Sid, 'Leave it Kuber, he has other friends too. I have met many of them over a game of cricket. Sid enjoys his time with whomsoever he is with.'

Kuber shrugs his shoulders, 'Well, I don't, for me it has been the pompous Prahlad and just the loyalty from you since primary school days.'

Yug says genuinely, 'Sid has always had a wider audience and a larger circle and group of friends to meet. I do not grudge or hold it against him. It is ingrained in his personality.'

Kuber finishes what he started, 'Well, I have to accept it as it is then. God riddance! If Sid is happier with other friends, then so be it. Let us head back home, otherwise the red marks on my cheeks will be harder than in my dad's mouth. Let me get him his paan.'

Kuber, talks to his schizophrenic self that night. Yet he is not self aware enough, as he does not see himself talking to himself. His mental health has suffered due to the unnatural events in his own family.

Kuber's elder sister has been married twice, and both her marriages had broken-up. Kuber blames his parents, more his father, talking to himself, '*He never gave her a choice in the first instance, and forced her into a second alliance.*' As he is brushing his teeth, he grinds them in angst.

Lying in bed, he watches the ceiling fan for a few minutes. '*The unhappiness of the situation for her, has come all over me. She is back home. What was the point? Why can she not stay and live with us permanently? She is also back with those same traumatic experiences, that mother has had to face.*'

As Kuber speaks to himself in anger, his voice trembles. He has developed this condition over a period of time, while living in his own family. It has been developing since he was eighteen, and has now bloomed fully into schizophrenia.

It is not his fault. His mother had taken things lying down. First, by not making Kuber's father understand, that their daughter was not ready for marriage. 'All women become ready, when they are in their husband's house. Were you ready to be in my bed?' he asks Kuber's mother. Kuber has overheard these conversations at the dining table, when his sister used to make that customary weekly call from USA. He used to wonder about his father's unnecessary gruff roughness.

His mother would repeat rhetorically. 'What was the need to send her so far away?'

'Can you keep a daughter in the same city as where you live?' would be the father's sting in return. Kuber would wince at these replies in his room continuing to remain in ear shot. He would wonder the nature of his own mother. '*Why can she not lead? Why can she not reply to father?*'

Kuber never understood these things, as his folks kept talking only to each other.

At nineteen, Kuber had began shaving, and asking himself a new set of questions, '*I cannot speak about sex education to my father. I cannot ask him for more money, than what my mother provides.*' He glumly led his life, day to day, but managed to whisk away his father's car. '*Father takes the train, the car remains parked in any case. I will park it back, before he returns, and mother will stay calm and quiet as well.*'

Kuber's mother began to plant a silent curtain over Kuber's stupid secrets, that he was behaviourally open to his mother. Yet, he never conceded a conversation to his mother. It was an understanding they two developed. Silent co-operation and co-existence.

When his sister was back home, after her second divorce, Kuber was in his fourth year of education. '*She does not need to hide, why is father being so mean to her?*' Kuber would rationalize to himself. Yet, he never confronted his mother, or stood up with her to his father. He remained in the background, listening and snooping into conversations.

At dining table conversations, the father would suggest to his daughter, 'Why don't you at least cook here, and relieve your mother? She is now sixty years old.' Their daughter would dutifully get up, and go silently from the dining table into the kitchen, where her mother would silence her with a finger on her own lips.

Kuber followed his mother's silence. Present in the mother's shadow, in the same space as his father, and retaining his position on the dining table, never himself going into the kitchen.

Kuber gradually became used to it, like a piece of furniture, and drew into his own silence. He would only ask himself at night while gargling on his Colgate mouth-wash, not even speaking aloud anymore, '*Am I not supposed to cook?*' The anger, flushed away as he peed silently.

'What matters is that I must never divorce, who want's this ol'man's ire? Who wants to return and live with him? I rather remain married, like him. He just punctures holes into the women at home.' His mind would talk to his inner self, and he would look into his own eyes in the mirror, accept the status quo, and gradually talk his own mental disorder into an order of life; a way of being.

An acceptance that his father was right gradually sunk in. 'Women were docile, at home, at college. They are merely objects of men's needs and satisfaction. Never to stand before a man, never to question, only to supply food, which they must. They want us to go and fetch food, hunt, bring back money and food. So they can run the house their way.'

His thoughts continued late that night, 'They can cook till we can eat to our hearts content. What else is there? Sex is available outside family life. Affections are just a body display of silly mannerisms. Look at my sister, twice married, twice to return. A return to the life of a rat, in a cat and dog house. The father barks, while our mother mews. Which girl that I marry will want to live with them?'

'It is as if, I am a jungle primate. The monkey on my bed in Matheran had it better. He had many more fellow monkeys as friends, who were in the room with their kids. There was more bonhomie in them. More like family friends. Free to jump from bed to bed, tree to tree. Live a free life. After all, what have we as a family become, if not a degenerated version of our ancestral apes?'

'Father does not have a friend, my sister does not have a friend. Do I have friends? Mother has her domestic maid as a friend. Aren't the monkeys better off?'

He sits before his mirror in the room, forlorn on his bed, thinking regressively, 'I love my friends more than I love Rekha. I could enjoy more with them sexually than with anyone. Perhaps more with the chiseled face Prahlad than with Yug. Yug is too tall. I can be the woman to Prahlad or Yug, naive and demure like my mother. I can hire a maid who would cook. At least my marriage will not fail.'

'I want to say no to Rekha, she does not understand all this, my tendencies, my love for other men. No one understands. Are they blind? Neither do the boys see it. They don't see it in my walk, my gait, my gaiety when I am with them. I wish I was my sister, given to another man. I would have made it work.'

Kuber gets up and locks his room from inside. He removes his clothes and stands nude before the full length mirror. He hopes to give himself pleasure.

He thinks of Rekha, and there is no arousal.

He thinks of Yug, and there is a bit of movement down under. He thinks of Prahlad with Yug, and moans to himself, 'Oh Yug, oh Prahlad, come!' before he can be fully aroused, he opens his eyes and looks at his ugly self in the mirror.

The arousal outside is over, the one inside is not satiated, as he feels it in his anal path.

He stops his failed masturbation act.

'Get wet all over at night again you foolish pecker,' he gazes at his slumping penis.

'I hate you, for who you are. I hate you for the family you are born in. I hate your father.' Kuber is oblivious that he is talking to himself, as if to a third person. Yet he makes no mistake to throw at himself the disdain that he has for his own father.

He enters the toilet, and has a piss. 'You can never be with a woman Kuber Savla. It will be a nightmare. She will realize, that you are not a man, someone who cannot get his serpent of desire up. You my friend, are an ape, who can copy others and live, but can live like a female monkey without children.'

He rubs his hand over his tummy. 'You can never have children, never impregnate a woman. How will you be fair to Rekha? How much will she take in her life with you?'

As he sits down back on his bed, he can visualize Prahlad and Yug laughing at him. He pops two aspirins and his sleeping medicine *Comppause*, obtained from his mother and sister's prescription. 'Dad is the only one who can get his sound sleep, the lucky bastard that he is. I wish I could poison him.'

The three tablets calm him down, and he eventually falls asleep.

The betel leaf paan, and the rat poison, is left abandoned at his side table.

10. Epigram

A Figure of Speech that makes a brief pointed saying by presenting antithetical ideas to arrest attention and surprise.

Illustration:
The material is immaterial.

10. Downhill

Few weeks later, Sid is surprised to see a marked difference in Rekha's scores after her revaluation comes in, and he shrugs at the level of the college they all study in.

Sid is talking to Yug, 'Life generally seems to be going downhill since moving out of school.' He expects the vibrant Yug to pep him up.

'It sucks, I dunno whats the point to study so hard.' exclaims Yug.

'You seem to be in the dole drums. What is the matter?' quizzes Sid.

Over lunch, Yug spills the beans and this has a very detrimental impact on Sid's friendship with Yug.

He is surprised that Yug tends to go back to his old loyalties without thinking about the repercussions on himself, his own career, and the impact of the wrong company that Kuber keeps that leads him to believe, that he can buy everything to get results.

Sid is concerned that this could drag Yug into a mess, and with him jeopardize the new alliance of warmth and trust that they had created with each other. The sheer madness of Kuber had been a known factor, but the unseen rashness of Yug's decision to associate himself with Kuber's schematics, scares Sid to believe, that he is better off by himself.

From the sixth semester in this third year, Sid begins to keep a low profile. He attends less of classes personally in college and spends more time in self-study and reference note gathering. Professors of the senior years, spend little time bothering about attendance and more about the grasp of their students and mastery of their subjects.

Sid also forms a stronger alliance with Dinshaw, and often meets Prahlad with his father once a year, to keep in touch and gain information about his progress and plans to visit overseas. He encourages Prahlad to chat and open up about his feelings.

Sid is surprised to find a broken dynamic between Prahlad and his father, and the loneliness of an over wealthy kid. Their family exerts wrong influences of each other on decision making and an over all sale of the soul; as long as opportunistic ideas can fly to gain further and make even more money. Sid feels lost seeing all this in Prahlad's life.

After all, Prahlad's family seems to be richer than what his next two generations could acquire in future, but Sid keeps a quiet watch and offers his friendship. He listens to Prahlad compassionately and offers his shoulder to cry on, willingly. Prahlad it appears has led a lonely life, raised by a maid in one corner of his house, an entirely different apartment to the next door apartment of his parents. Sid finds this very hard to digest, that they live practically separately in their respective spaces, with just dinner time chitter chatter.

His time spent with Dinshaw opens up Sid's social life to another dozen new friends, competitive Bombay gully cricket matches and binge watching MTV videos and billboard top hits. They spend their summer vacations collecting songs lists streaming out of the USA, by visiting small recording studios that convert music from original master tapes, into blank TDK and Sony cassettes.

Music and sport open up a refreshing world of what a simple de-stressed life can be; and Sid enjoys his time to the hilt.

Sid and Dinshaw collectively unite their area friends, to make a cricket team and compete with other apartment blocks in friendly fixtures – that makes them believe, that '*Jo Jeeta Woh Sikander*' is really not a film, but a moniker to find their true way of life, sport and bonhomie with love in times ahead.

Friends like Kriplani, Sharma and even Mukesh enjoy their cricket and bird watching together, often cracking crass and funny jokes together, trying to involve Sid and Dinshaw with them.

Sid also comes to realize what true love is, and decides not to chase girls, but wait and see, if any girl takes an interest in him. The waiting game is what girls usually play, and Sid does not find any true merit in going after any of the girls in his college, after an early fiasco. One of his love interests, finds herself engaged in less than six months after a break-up in his Architecture college.

Sid takes deep interest in a girl called Simi who comes into his life from a series of common family friends, and begins to introduce her to his friends like Prahlad and Yug, after Kuber and Rekha bump into them at Hill Road. 'It was not a date, but just a meal outdoors,' he clarifies to Yug.

He wishes to openly circulate and check out their joint social interests and how all the friends also take to her.

Kuber takes to this girlfriend of Sid and keeps egging Rekha on to connect with her, or take life lessons from her. Kuber broaches these topics with Rekha each time they are together much to the discomfort of Simi, who prefers the company of Yug and Prahlad as Sid's friends.

Sid's cautious yet open and optimistic approach leads to joint parties, 3-6pm film shows and a different kind of bonding of four of them meeting more often together, as couples.

Prahlad and Yug continue to remain single, awkward and gawky. Simi lives before his friends with the same causal spirit, as Sid and Simi's other social groups.

Sid compares their relationship often to a brownie, sizzling hot and soft on the inside, melting and sweet to taste, but difficult for their worlds to digest.

When Kuber probes, they both deflect it to some 'silly family opposition.' It seems like a deep crust pizza filled with cheese to me,' jokes Simi. They don't feel like opening up their pandora's box entirely before Kuber.

'Lots of mozzarella cheese in the centre then,' counters Sid often to her. Their banter, keeps Kuber curious, as to what makes them tick, and soon, he notices that he is no longer the centre of attention on campus, nor is he Rekha's world.

Younger junior students begin to queue up before Rekha to ask her for design and drawing help. Her ability to have bounced back after carrying over three to four subjects as a backlog into the next year and finally clearing over eleven subjects in her seventh semester, all together makes her popular on campus.

It is a success story that even Batumal Thodani has never seen before.

Kuber whose roving eye follows many a girl, still maintains his love life with Rekha successfully. This, while his envious self, is tailing Sid all over college to keep track of his activities on campus, and in the cinema halls with Simi.

He begins to mirror Sid's life following him, keeping tabs, and generally observing all sorts of smaller nuances, which he fails to replicate in his own relationship. Yet he continues to measure, to compare and yet does not mean badly for *all* others.

Kuber has never seen this kind of love, loyalty and likeness to each other, with a long term intent that he observes in Sid for Simi and vice versa. 'Is he really so blessed? Let's find out some day from his beloved.'

After hacking many a plan, and aborting all of them, time runs out for Kuber, and they all graduate as Architects.

Only Kuber and Sid have remained steady, in a relationship all through college. Yug is happy with his single status, while Prahlad works hard to fight off his awkwardness.

On the eve of their results being released for USA Masters entrance examinations, and them securing their Architecture degrees, news of Kuber breaking Rekha's heart hits them all. The desire for a break-up before flying to a new location is Kuber's way of breaking free from his past.

Prahlad calls Sid at night, 'No one else will tolerate his nonsense and stay committed with Kuber. What with all his duality, manipulation and meanness. Can you talk some sense into him, if not yourself, via or with Rekha and Simi?'

'Well, Rekha used to find him charming, what exactly happened?' says an irritated Sid into his house phone speaker.

'Well, the material is immaterial.' Prahlad is hinting at Kuber going overseas.

Sid, in his explanatory tone, 'You always say that Prahlad, because you have always had everything taken care of. Your education here and abroad. Your sneakers, your clothes, your car. Don't throw that at Kuber, else he will throw your 28 inch TV at you.'

'Okay, okay! Yug says Kuber has told him that he has found another girl. Yug is right in the centre of it, as Rekha has fainted twice in college and Yug had to help her to be put in a cab to send her home.'

'Oh I see, I did not know.' says Sid, 'I never took additional interest in another's personal life, till being asked to.'

'You all were on the same campus in Mumbai, were you not?' asks a curious Prahlad. 'We must figure out what is happening?'

'I don't go to college every day these days as we are just finishing our final project presentations and preparing only for the viva's,' replies Sid.

'I have called a gathering of just five of us. Sarkaar is also in town as he and I both are done with our vivas. He is staying with me.' Prahlad knows, that he can rope in Sid now that Som Sarkaar is in town.

'That's nice of you,' responds Sid. He always appreciates any kindness he can see from Prahlad, despite fighting his own demons.

'I am turning into a new leaf, at least trying to.' says Prahlad.

Sid, still circumspect, 'Why am I needed? I would not want to intervene with Kuber due to our history. All of us together again after so many years, it is a potent combination.'

Prahlad pushes Sid, 'Only you with your blunt frankness and openness can dig something out of Kuber.'

Sid, with a wry smile on his face, speaks into the speaker of his home wired phone, 'My mere presence will make him feel uncomfortable, as all four of us have spent a lot of time together.'

'That is exactly why, try to use it to our advantage. Let us try once to thaw him out.' Prahlad cajoles without pleading.

'Okay, you seem to be pretty convinced. I will pick Yug up on the way. I'll connect with Yug. See you at eight.'

Later that night, Yug enters the front seat of Sid's dad's car when he honks below his home at the corner shop, 'Some *Chikki* Sid-Paaji?' Jaggery peanut square shaped bites are Sid's favourite delight.

Sid lets out his trademark wry smile and picks a piece, 'Yuggy you always remember. Thanks Pal.'

Yug chips in, 'I should thank you, for all the pickup drops and cyclostyling, and all the bourbon you picked for me. We need you tonight.'

'Love you man. Will miss the old college days. Try to keep good company Yug.' advises Sid.

'I still miss the school days,' rues Yug. 'It all got over so fast. If we break away tonight, I know Kuber and Prahlad since our kindergarten. There is no turning back.'

'What is up with Kuber?' Asks Sid as he shifts gears in the Maruti 800 car too.

Yug claims, 'Oh he is full of excuses; he has given different reasons to his mother at home, who is worried and keeps calling my mum, he has different excuses for Rekha, who has been sobbing for past three days, and a completely different justification to me. Which one do you want to hear?'

'All three!' chimes Sid.

He winks at Yug, acknowledging for a minute, that 'Don't we all know Kuber.' *thats a Matheran kinda moment* look on Sid's face.

'Well, his mother says he is not keen to get married, as he wants to explore USA first.'

Yug watches Sid intently for a response, as Sid observes the expectant expression on Yug's face silently. Sid nods, to egg him on.

Yug goes on, 'Rekha says he has broken up with her, because he is dating some new girl in Colaba who resides in his Masi's building, but the story sounds unbelievable and the girl's data, points to his own cousin.'

Sid mime's a Prahlad kind of expression, making Yug smile a bit. 'Is the immaterial, material? Why you getting so serious? It's Kuber's life you are getting too intertwined with.'

'And to me, he says, that he finds himself incompatible with Rekha completely. Which one to believe?' Yug is exasperated, and falls backwards from the edge of his seat in the car. He takes his hands and strongly brushes his hair back, as if their order has been disturbed beyond any combing cure.

'Well, none really. If I know Kuber well, all three reasons are lies.' Sid smiles looking ahead over the dashboard.

Sid maintains his pleasant disposition, understanding and remaining understated, that perhaps *Kuber has got overwhelmed with his own self.*

Yug just stares on at Sid, 'That is a bit too much Sid, even though I know, you know Kuber better instinctively.'

'You have a better explanation?' queries Sid. 'You know him since ten more years than me, so you should figure him out better.' Sid knows Yug will now not challenge Sid, as he remains unclear in his perception of Kuber's seriousness. Or the lack of it. Yug just does not judge, it is not that he is a poor judge of bad character, heart of heart, he knows Kuber the best.

'No, replies Yug?' asks Sid, as they walk into Prahlad's home.

Sarkaar has a smirk and a funny expression, to which Sid tells him, 'Don't look so overjoyed, we are not here to celebrate; your exams are over, we know we know.'

Prahlad sits on the sofa and asks, 'Come on, spill the beans quickly'

They share each other's rationale and wait for their childhood buddy to enter.

As Prahlad and Sid discuss their conspiracy theories, Sarkaar watches intently, but is non commital and silent. Yug is too taken aback with so many permutations and combinations. It tires him to feel sleepy, when the door bell rings.

The servant boy at Prahlad's house announces Kuber's entry.

'Come come Kuber.' speaks out Prahlad, and lays the cards on the table so that no one deflects and wastes time to corner Kuber. Yug has ensured that Rekha's perspective gets the first preference and he lays his version of her information on the table.

'Rekha must be heart broken. After all, with her modest background, the material is after all very very material.' Prahlad's sarcastic cynicism does not get anyone's goat, but it leaves no room for doubt, what he thinks of Rekha.

Sid does not seem amused. 'The material is only immaterial to you Prahald. Not everyone can afford even their India fees for their Masters. So let's not go there.'

Kuber with his large toad eyes, is amused and looks at them all with a smile, that is neither wicked nor deliberate. It almost appears planned and calculative on Kuber's part. He seems to enjoy to keep them all guessing about his life- making himself the centre of attraction. 'I am just exiting the country and one phase of life, to open another. I do not want to carry baggage.'

'For once why don't you tell us your real truth, rather than spin multiple yarns. Or are we too baggage now?' quips Sid.

Yug clarifies, as if to classify Prahlad in the same superiority category, before the insecurity in him makes Prahlad feel like a lower mortal. 'Clearly Prahlad is not, he is joining you to the USA.'

Sarkaar and Sid exchange their looks as if they were inside the Matheran toy train, waiting to get out for excitement and some fun. 'Haven't we all seen enough?' asks Sarkaar simply.

Kuber speaks up, 'Let us then each go our ways. Without judgement and fear, without friendship or care. Embrace the world.'

'What about our joint plans to visit Goa next week, before you leave? Prahlad and I have already booked our tickets.' Yug spills the beans.

'I have to go to Baroda,' says Sarkaar. 'No one told me the dates, as always, I am looped out.'

Sid interjects, 'I never confirmed, as I have plans with Simi, who is flying out to Bangalore.'

'Let us leave it, for another time,' says Prahlad. 'Just you and I won't be fun.' He comforts the disappointed Yug, not realizing that he is hurting Yug's feelings.

'You think everything else through Kuber, except your relationships, you cannot just flick on and off with people like a switch when you wish to think you make merry, and are cheerful, and you drop people and friends like a hot potato when you deem fit. Is this fair to Rekha?' Sid makes the claim more like an affirmation rather than a conversation or a question.

He places no guilt on Kuber, but paints him with the brush of selfishness and irresponsibility a terrible combination which his other friends do not seem to be observant about.

'What is it to you?' answers Kuber rudely.

He talks to himself, muttering, out of audible zone from his friends, he paces in the room, 'I wish I could kill him.' Kuber remembers his fathers night conversations with his mother, and is troubled by it.

Prahlad speaks genuinely from his heart, 'That is not an answer to my question, our question? Be open and truthful to us at least.'

'That's what friends are for,' says a concerned Yug.

'A friend indeed.' Sid's manner of sarcastic speech is not so obvious.

'Goals over girls.' shrugs Kuber loudly. Each of them fall into a muted silence.

Kuber grins to himself, 'Can they ever understand, what I am going through?' he mutters, and gradually stutters, 'Mf#@*.er' and collapses on the sofa chair.

'Girls? It is just Rekha we are talking about,' says a confused Yug. Drawn as he is by others emotions, Yug is now severely entangled with both his shoulders dropping.

Yug imagines that on his one shoulder he has Rekha sobbing in absentia, the other has Prahlad using it like an emotional crutch since secondary school. Yug can see imaginary blurbs and cloud captions all around his head, like swarming bees.

He imagines them in the form of a blurb each time he has to speak or decide as a group of friends. He falls silent.

'Yug, don't lose focus, we are not here just due to Rekha. We are asking Kuber a palatable reason for his own decision and his life. Why does he think he is doing what he is doing?' Sid has spoken suggestively.

'*I just want to break-free*. Like Freddy Mercury. What is our peer group going to achieve? Are we expected to carry this friendship deep into adulthood or old age?' Kuber offers his biggest hint, on his own queerness.

Sid baulks at the hint, and is about to question what it implies, but no words leave his mouth.

'You should have thought that before getting entangled.' Sarkaar finally loses his cool. 'All our outings or get togethers are only about Prahlad or Kuber. You all are so lucky and well provided, you neither had to leave the comforts of your homes, and live in a hostel, where there is more water in your cafeteria's tea, than in the river Godavri. Try boarding a train from Sholapur station. You feel you are coming from the morass of emptiness and death, into a city of high density where people are crammed like cockroaches. And then, all this, this...unpleasantness at such a young age for the girl.'

Without shouting, or getting upset in his dead-pan expression, Kuber responds clinically 'I don't owe any of you an explanation about my love life. Just fuck off!'

'Next time don't combine your day to day events like a gang or troupe then. Live your life buddy – all by yourself.' Yug is now in disgust, he looks toward Sid, who remains quiet.

'That's what I have been doing my infant terrible.' jokes Kuber nonchalant and unaffected.

Sid feels like getting up and beating him up. Yet he displays self-control and knows he would reduce him to pulp in minutes with Prahlad lacking the strength and Yug the conviction to stop him. Sarkaar would only be too pleased. He has also sensed Kuber's own self disgust.

Sid wants to disconnect from a person, who does not like his own self enough to justify being a friend to him. He gets up to leave, 'I am going home' he says.

Prahlad claims, 'Perhaps you are not ready to leave for America? Are you merely following me? Imitation is a cheap copy, an expensive experiment.'

'Go figure, fucker;' says Kuber and walks out before Sid.

11. Alliteration

A figure of speech where the repetition of the same sound, or <u>letter</u> at the beginning of the words in a phrase

Illustration:
Not reading between the <u>L</u>ines of the <u>L</u>etters taken <u>L</u>iterally in <u>L</u>ondon, it <u>l</u>eads him to the <u>L</u>ocation in <u>L</u>orlim, where he <u>L</u>ost his <u>L</u>ove.

(<u>Letters</u> of the friends follow...)

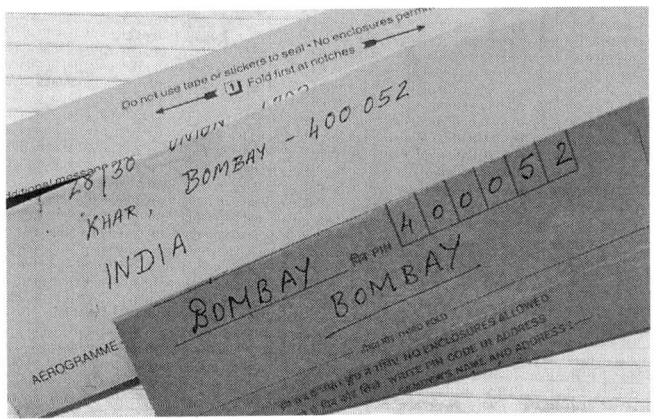

11. Letters over the years

November 28th '93

TO PRAHLAD, FROM SID (1993)

Dear Prahlad,

Yo Man! I called your residence, and someone by the name of Catherine picked up the phone. And she was like, Prahlad is not there like, he is down under like, I mean....like...; who the hell is she? Sounds like a hippy from the 70's.

Someone living in with you pal? Or just a room partner? You don't say, like...!!!

Anywayzzz man, here's wising you a Happy Birthday! Wishing ! I hope you like, wisen up!

Thought of writing a letter to you, as you were complaining about the lack of any letter from your folks. Grow up dude. Maybe your father has so many responsibilities, that he thinks you have become mature and all grown up.

Well, he should have checked with us, ha ha.

We have to discount our parents too pal, maybe they went through a lot when they were separated from their home land, and migrated to Bombay...cut them some slack?

Do you believe in the Hindu Dharma of re-birth and the cycle of events and actions? Karma can take you into your new life, maybe you are born human or animal again next time? Perhaps our folks were all born elsewhere in London or New York before they were reborn in India. You are the lucky chosen one who won his lottery to Americaaaa! So enjoy that life you chose pal.

I do acknowledge that your father could have made your life easier, by understanding what you wanted. But then once you study so much, he may have also expected, that you wish to live your own life? I dunno your family dynamics, but each of us are exploring life in different directions, though we came from the same school. So the same may have happened with our dads, and knowing that he has still let you choose your own destiny. Not that he had other options, I know, I know -you would not easily listen to him.

I for one, do not have the courage of my convictions to step out and go and live so far away from my family at twenty two. I love my parents, and though dad thinks I am taking life too easy, he was surprised that I stayed back and studied in Bombay itself.

Got to know from you about your sister's life and it is sad that it has not worked out. Pooja was such an intelligent girl with all the smarts. She should certainly practice her medicine. I am sure with her separation now, and her further studies, she will be able to grow into a mature profession in one of the hospitals around New Jersey.

You do not worry too much and live your life.

My sister has rejected proposals from over a dozen boys, including three of them who really suited and liked her. We cannot understand what she is looking for. Sometimes in an arranged match, the two people do not click after the initial few meetings. Well, that's what she tells me.

Sometimes girls have a complex about strange things, and at times the boys who have come to see her, have acted like creeps. So it is difficult to get into an arranged marriage scenario, and perhaps as their younger brothers we are lucky.

We can learn form their life and their choices and mistakes. Sometimes younger siblings just choose differently due to that. Don't you think so?

However, I do feel you are making the same mistake as our sisters. Both of our siblings are elder to each of us. Let me explain.

Our sisters never mingled with friends and socialized, nor travelled after university. Those was the 1980's - simple and conservative times.

It would have changed their entire perspective of life and their selection of their partner could have been very different. I am involved in listening to what my sister has to talk, and yet go out and buy the requisite sweets, to table over every cup of tea, when boys come over with their families to see her.

Would I ever be able to go through such a process? So awkward! A girl has to consider so many suitors and proposals and then make do with the choice she is stuck with. That's what little I understood from Kuber too, when he would talk about his family.

The concept of dating in India is so different from America. Living in as room partners is just not an option.

We do not seem to be in a hurry to jump into bed; girls are not so eager, and mushy and the pop culture of America has yet to entirely land on our shores.

Look at cricket, Kapil Dev was just twenty four years old when he won the World Cup for India. You were a big aficionado for cricket. Take inspiration from that. Win something. You were always competitive in school and college. What has happened now? Why aim so low?

I am sure you will also get us the coveted masters degree from Cincinnati, something all us friends will be proud of. So chin up and be happy buddy, as you are living the life of your choice ultimately. Your dreams, your life.

Your dad and family will always be where it is, waiting for you. I do however agree, migrating like this has its own challenges, but birds also fly back home, during the mating season;-) so I am sure you too can do that. Time it.

As you say, ultimately an Indian wife, will be more adjustable with you. So you are right there. You truly have not Americanized but then you truly not Indianized either. So where do you belong?

Live in India at that time with your green card or citizenship.

I seem to believe that I will live and die an Indian. It appears the same with Yug too, he is even more die-hard Indian than I am. Sarkaar is on another planet all together in Mohenjo Daro era, it appears with his archaic ideas but very rooted values. He is a pure traditionalist. I accepted that about him long back.

So, we three are happy to hear you are wrapping up your Master's degree.

You after all have been the most intelligent from our group, (after me;-);-) and have gotten to study further in America now. I hope all your American dreams come true. Kuber is not so clued in with us, and does not call, nor write often. I hope to hear in detail from you as you said you prefer letter writing.

Referring to your conversation with me on my birthday that just went past, yes I too am happy pursuing a masters degree. MBA is a good program and India is really opening up to all Multinational companies, so our work plans here should be fine. We may earn all of five hundred dollars, but our expenses are not over a couple of hundred.

My friend, your love life? Hope you stop looking for Raveena Tandon? Lower your benchmark pal, do not give looks so much importance, see the person's human qualities as they come back to bite you later. (Ask Rekha!)

You Sagittarius people make friends easy, but it is tough to hold on to you guys, as your own loyalties are fleeting and fast flying for others.

I am sure you do not have such thick friends like us in America.

Did we overstep with Kuber before he flew out? I always felt so. Perhaps he was unsure and got huddled into a relationship in college life, that he did not feel like honouring her all his life.

Sometimes we give our heart away too easily. You seem to be on the other end of the spectrum.

So remember, time will run out. All the lovely Indian ladies will be taken.

More in my next, and Yug says we need to receive you at the airport if you fly down for new year eve.

I suggest you take a cab bugger. See you on the other side of the new year.

Cheers, Sid.

Ψ

TO SID, FROM YUG (1999)

7th November'99

Dear Sid,

How are you doing in London? I am sure by now you must be well settled with Simi and explored all the sights around Wales and Scotland.

It was nice of you to send me your entire music collection, locally from India for my birthday.

At twenty nine, it does make me feel like nineteen again. All the memories of college life, dance parties and Bombastic outings in Bombay with you at *R.G.'s, Avalon, and the Razzberry Rhinoceros* come rushing back. I just no longer visit these places, but the music collection you have sent me, takes me there mentally and transcends me to our earlier world.

How carefree our times were!

I treasure the music as much as you, and will keep it carefully till you return, if you ever do. Sold your soul to the British Queen haven't you? Don't worry, the music labels, CDs will all be in fine shape with me.

I believe you had a nice trip to Genting and Cameroon Highlands, and found some British relics there. I remember my Malaysian and Singapore friends a lot, but have managed to find a foothold in my life as I am back where I belong. The money is good, and I feel Bombay's vibe where we all grew up.

So I came out of the Lah-Lah land in good time. Those peanut gravy satays and laksa were so good. You would have loved the Tiger beer more than your Budweiser you keep gulping down.

Let us plan a trip to Goa, if you are back for the holidays next summer. You may have to make it before that as I am seeing girls for marriage via a marriage bureau. The Goa trip has been pending since college. Do not let go so much that a short vacay is not possible?

Looking forward to some Walker's short bread and the China made magnet souvenirs you can carry back on your next trip; what else is there in UK?

They looted us, and now you must plunder them and get all your wealth back. Help me select my girl, and then you can go back to Great Britain if you like.

Yet I feel our life here will be better as couples. The wives should get along I hope.

Chal buddy, more when we meet. I am sure you are making good money and will foray into business as you have planned. You are right about the y2K software bugs, and your company seems to be milking it.

Yet the threat to that phenomena will be the start of e-commerce as companies start moving things on-line they could discover that hardware will become obsolete, and software will control the world.

Say hi to Simi and good luck to you, until we meet in Y2k.

From Bandra Bombay, your school '*chaddi buddy*', never gonna grow up, never gonna give you up! (remember Rick Astley)

Yours truly,
H.D.I
(High Definition Intent friend,

YugDharamjit Ikani - hee hee!)

Ψ

TO SID, FROM KUBER (2001)

14th March   **Kuber Savla, Bom-52, India.**

Dear Sid,

I hope you get this aerogramme in the snail mail in time before your holidays to Paris.

Here is a vote of thanks from me, for my birthday cake sent by you and Prahlad. Hats off to you guys to remember my birthday, despite me missing yours often.

Yug came over and we spent some old days time together gossiping about you both, and yeah, we agreed, you were more intelligent, though you cared less.

Prahlad was always more intense.

Prahlad's father seems to have invested my money on his name, and it appears I am foolish to have sunk my investments with them.

Sarkaar keeps calling Yug locally and telling him it is a big mistake to have gotten into business together. So did Yug who burnt his fingers and money with Prahlad himself.

I guess it is some way of twisted *guru-dakshina* we are incurring. What for, when they have been so wealthy all their life? They should be better experienced in business. Or are they not happy to see anyone else make more money and progress?

I am sure you are making truckloads of it in your business now in London. Big move in the dot com bust, to have ventured out on your own. Suits you well to have called your services business 'WeFix' when you are right now a one man startup. Who's the 'We?'

Do look ahead, and think about investing in Goa with me; I have chosen a brilliant site near Colva beach, and it will easily allow us to build twelve villas. A beach facing house in India is a dream the middle-class will buy, and we could build the next complex and gated community, with greens, trees, clean air. Peace and serenity.

As discussed during Yug's marriage, it could be your second innings and allow for a homecoming.

Rekha and I are trudging along, no kids – so empty nest always.

The patch-up with her, was to settle down with someone I already knew, as other options in America did not really work out, finally we both decided to return to India and create my business here. It's a natural progression as an architect for me to design and own my projects.

Mum keeps giving me grief, wheres' the family? My sister stress has been there, since she returned to India she is better off being next door with the folks.

Though she does not get a break from our parents, there is no other way. Your sister is expecting monetary help now, when you are yet to make your own house in London? I am sure her brother will send her truckloads of it, to buy her the house she wants, but do watch out from your brother in law, I have met him in India on common friends outings.

He does not seem to have his bearings right. Something seems off.

Prahlad's life story is the same in New Jersey.

All our sisters married men, who are neither like our fathers, in terms of self-esteem, nor modern and educated well enough like us, to have achieved things on their own merit.

I set the cops loose on my sister's first husband for him ill-treating her and even locking up her passport when she lived in Philly. Rekha bore the brunt of it when we lived in America.

We are experimenting this year, as I had to relocate to India, spreading my investments on outskirts of Bombay and to procure the Goa land. Rekha joins me soon, as I do feel lonely, yet someone between us two has to do the hard work of earning a salary, and it is her for now.

We have packed up our home, and she is currently living out of hotels, with no overload of running a home day to day. I am living again like a bachelor with my parents.

Maybe next year, when I fly back to New York to join her, I will stop by in London and look you up. Yug says your family home is large enough to allow me to stay put for a few days.

We can rev up our plans for Goa and make a travel trip together too, if you agree, it could be just the two of us and we can ask Yug to join in the second leg. He is not keen to invest jointly. Thinks only of himself and his own family.

I have been reminding him to procure something in Bombay as it will get unaffordable later, but he is as risk averse as Sarkaar. What kind of friends these are, who do not trust their own friend and invest to make a simple house together?

I am sure you are different.

Sarkaar is still living in his old family home close to the railways, and he criss crosses in travel all over the city. The house will not be worth living in after a few years once his daughter grows up.

Each one to their own, I share my views openly to you as you listen. Prahlad and Yug no longer do, after their short experiment and failure in business. They seem to have burnt each other's fingers.

Let us do something together, that binds our old memories and bonhomie together. Business and money will always be a by product of our hard work.

It is one life. Live fully.

Looking for your support,
Kuber the *mastikhor* (The Mischievous one)

Ψ

TO KUBER, FROM SID (2004)

26th January 2004

Dear Kuber,

Suresh in USA is my ex-colleague and plans to set up our business in America, it will be our London subsidiary.

Feel free to participate in taking up a share. That way you and I can have a passive investment in America and still have a majority share for decision making.

I have been in business now for just about four years, but it is all very new for Suresh, specially the audit part.

Your Goa plans have still not fructified, so there is no chance to invest there, I can loan you some money as an investment in India, but I thought you were not keen any further to do business with Prahlad's father.

I hear differently from Prahlad.

As far as I am concerned, it will be a hedge to America and real estate in Bombay can never go south.

You have promised an interest return of over twelve percent, that is good for me, but I will need the money back once we are in India.

Simi and I are expecting our second child, so we should be home toward the end of the year...yes, that's the good news from me.

If everything falls in place, you will have your dream of doing some business, with one of us from our school days.

I know you are disappointed by the others, but they are in jobs now and have a different mindset so it is better you accept that.

Yug is rightly conservative and Sarkaar has always been a traditionalist, so totally against mixing business things in friendship.

I do feel Yug would have been a genuine gem to do something with us, but it is not meant to be.

Prahlad has become a loner. He does not get to do things with his own father, so where is the question of being bound in business with us both.

He has his family baggage to bear.

Let us take one step at a time, and reach a stage of happiness and contentment too. Please do not see it as a mid-life crisis, instead you should feel life is an oasis.

Friendship gives us all solace in a dark isolated world.

Yug was rightly suggesting adoption for you and Rekha. If you raise a kid, you will not feel isolated. Every friend is also looking for different things so don't feel disappointed, some day we all will land up in Goa in your hotel.

Time is limited my friend, our hearts must keep the space for each other.

Yug tells me, you seem to have no time for family on your hands, so you declined his child-like suggestion on the conference call the other day.

It does bind the marriage Kuber, so think about it, as you seem to miss kids more than Rekha. You are good with them too, our son, see's you like a real relative.

When we meet on your trip via Heathrow, I shall see you outside the terminal T2, at 7 in the evening.

With your passport you should be able to step out for a while.

Chat with you then, *Sidey* days are here again;-);-) monkeys let loose in London!

Cheers,

Sid.

12. Synecdoche

A figure of speech, that substitutes the part, to signify the whole.

Illustration:
'...this is the last tranche I am sending to India.'

12. The Final Call

September 5, 2006 is the date of the final call.

A call between an ambitious husband, and a busy wife. There is also an announcement at the airport for the final boarding call for Rekha's flight.

Kuber is back home in India, living in with his parents at the ripe old age of thirty five. He finds himself amidst his sister's declining visibility and his folks disparate way of being.

Kuber calling his wife long distance at mid-night from his bachelor bedroom, 'Rekha, I need you to sign the papers jointly. We finally have a house we can buy and live in. I cannot keep paying the rent like this.'

He awaits a response, as a voice-over trails into his ear-piece, 'The Delta flight DL 5187 from JFK airport is on time, and will depart in thirty minutes from gate C93.'

Standing under the signage of the gate #93, is a harassed Rekha awaiting departure for her ERP software training to Toronto.

Rekha responds, 'Why are you over investing in India? I will like to eventually live in America, it will be easier for me. When there are no parents, what will we do there? What will we do with so much investment there?'

When choices differ, decisions collide and conflict grows.

'You don't understand, 'coz you are not here. India is a lot more easier to live in.' explains Kuber.

He continues, 'We too will age, and need domestic help, medical care and what not. We are all living here, to simply light their pyres. Who will light ours?'

'I am sending dollars every month to India, and continuing to just over extend myself here. We can always move into a commune' she replies.

She does not have family or children on her mind, as she has to prepare for an examination for her software certification. 'I have software patch work to do tonight, and there is no space for me to think.'

'Well, you choose to live by yourself in hotel rooms. Anyway, that was always the plan.' He continues to stutter and mutters below his breath, more talking to himself than her, as if to demand a ransom from his schizophrenic self.

'But the plan was never to keep adding my money to your business,' interjects Rekha.

'Rekha, forget the past, this is for our own house. The money taken from you will all come back to you eventually. For whom am I doing all this?' chides a angsty Kuber.

'Certainly not for me, I am happy in America,' comes Rekha's flat reply.

'Your own father is falling sick repeatedly, last trip you were here, you were unhappy living out of hotels. You were unhappy living with my parents, you can't live with your own folks. Where can you live? You are getting too used to living with yourself in America.'

There is silence from the other side. Kuber has been blunt. Perhaps there is some truth in that.

Rekha does not know how to respond, so she shuts down, like the college days.

She is waiting, that he will wish her on her birthday. Her feelings talk to her. 'It has become a marriage of convenience and needs. Only his.'

She recovers, 'Kuber, this is the last tranche I am sending to India. It will take me five more years to earn the same money back post taxes. Remember, after this house, no more money going into property or your business, which is just a dark hole for me that I cannot understand.' Exasperated, Rekha is deep breathing on the other side of the planet, where it is still Sept 5th.

Kuber demands, 'Yes madam, now send the electronic transfer to State Bank of India. I have put in the account details over the email to your yahoo account.'

Rekha justifies, 'It will be there in two days. Give me a day tomorrow, as I am in transit on my way to...'

He cuts her off, 'Okay, talk to you soon.' he puts the phone down, and mutters to himself, 'I took her there, re-educated her, got her trained and certified with my salary, and now she thinks no end of herself. Does not understand that we will need a roof over our own heads.'

'Oh Kuber!' she thinks to herself at the gate before boarding from the JFK Intl. Airport. 'Is it too late? Can you not see? We want different things and are just drifting apart.'

Drained from all energy, she walks up with her boarding pass to the check-in crew in the priority line for business passengers.

Their priorities have completely changed.

Rekha knows what direction things are headed, as she boards her plane.

13. Sept. 10th 2007

'Hey, Guruji. Are we meeting today evening?' Sarkaar is excited with a gleam in his eyes. He awaits the answer from the other side of the phone.

'Sure Sarkaar. It is your birthday, we will obviously meet. Your favourite restaurant in Vile Parle?' clarifies Sid.

'Oh yes,' quips an excited Som Sarkaar. 'I thought you are visiting your folks from London, you will not have time.'

Sid asks, 'Have you not outgrown this? Is Yug joining? We have been there like a hundred times.'

Sarkaar is shaking his head, 'No, and no. I must get my share of the South Indian savouries. Yug has no time, he is working over time even on Saturday. These tech companies give you no breathing space.'

'Yug was very keen to meet you as well, perhaps he prefers one on one with you.'

'Sid, the group dynamics have never worked. You held us together. Once you and Simi went away to London, the friendship dried out.'

Sid tries again to convince him otherwise, thinking of taking his friend to a slightly better place, 'It is a Gujarati management restaurant. You want to eat south Indian food? Indian is Indian! We can go to a better place where we can sit for longer, later end up at a cafe.'

'How does that matter, it is still cheap! I don't like all that drama. Simple food is good enough. A nice Mumbai cutting-chai later for you my London Boy! I would love to see you have street food. Remember, I do not have tea, nor coffee.' replies Sarkaar.

'Cheapo, remember I am the one treating, and you must then go back walking after lunch,' laughs Sid.

'That is why my friend, I am happy in that much, as always you will pick me up, and I will walk back home. I do not want my friend to waste his money and fuel in taking u-Turns on our roads. Since Yug is not joining, some idli-dosa is good enough for both of us. Just like old times in the school cafeteria.'

'Ok, see you in ten minutes.' Sid agrees, and wonders aloud, 'When will this guy change?'

'Perhaps never,' replies his wife Simi.

He looks up at her, and she just gazes and smiles back at him. Marital bliss thy name is Simi.

'To real friends, old places matter, new hot shot places don't. Enjoy the day with him you can't turn back the clock, but you can sure count on Sarkaar. Re-collect his birthday message for you on your birthday Sid.'

Sid quips back, 'Yeah – he says I have always been there for people, and not allowed them to fall. It is a sort of pressure too. I know him since childhood, he is still a child at heart.

His nature has been ram-rod straight, while we used to rib him being roly-poly in school. At times square in the head. But very clean and straight in his friendship.' Sid recalls the Matheran memories, but does not verbalize them to Simi.

'Luck you,' says Simi, as she stands at the door to wave good-bye, 'You have many loved ones.'

'It is strange, I always felt closest to Yug, during college days – yet Yug felt closer to Prahlad, who was the closest to Kuber. That explains Prahlad and Kuber's American dreams. Me, Yug and Sarkaar were deeply Indian, simple wants, no desires; Sarkaar always idolized me, and I hoped to just be there for him, so that he does not get bullied. Kuber was fond of us all, and sometimes none at all. He lived his life more for himself.'

Sid had summed up his four decades association in a few lines.

Simi corrected Sid, 'That fellow was always opportunistic, living only for himself.'

Sid, in his flow, 'He was looking for love, rather than wait to let love find him. That is the thing about love and death, they find you.'

'Why do you have to be pragmatic and poetic at the same time?' Simi questions to stop Sid.

'A dark romantic. Fact is nothing lasts forever, only love will survive rebirth. You are born with your nature. For some cynicism survives rebirths, for me it will be romanticism.'

'You are a class apart, that's why I married you, your spirit conquered my heart.' Simi places her head on his shoulder.

14. Rhetorical Question

A figure of speech, which is without a question mark, and does not necessitate an answer.

Illustration:

'Who would not like to be in your place. What more can you ask for.'

14. E-Mail

Email:
to; Sid@Wefix.com
from: PrahladIsGod@USAisbest.com
Date: December 19, 2010

Dear Sid,

Happy Anniversary! It has been years since your marriage.

You lucky man, you lucked out, married to your sweetheart Simi, two kids Simran and Sid, a suburban life in London. *Who would not like to be in your place.*

I see with envy your snaps on FB with your parents visiting you and going for holidays to Scotland, Wales, everywhere in the countryside.

What more can you ask for. God bless you!

As I had suggested I am sure the train ride from Kings Cross must have been super enjoyable. Did you find the car ride through the meadows in Wales to be more appealing? Or was the train ride through Leeds more exciting?

The Royal Mile in Edinburgh does give you the impression that you are in some old Gothic city; as if elves and whacky old Scottish men will come out with their bagpipers. What bagpiper meant to us both in college days? Lovely memories...

Did you enjoy the Scottish gin? It is supposed to be world famous. As much if not more, as their Scotch. Or you now a dry fruit ol'fella?

I wish I was there with you at Lords. Hope to catch a cricket series sooner than later with you ol'pal.

How's the fitness regime? I see Simi post some hot snaps of hers, where are you man? Waiting on her outside in the car I guess, on your conference calls.

Do check if she has some hot cousin tucked away somewhere in India, I fail to find a match on all these western dating sites.

One mad capper than another. I am sure you must be rubbing your hands in glee, you scored and out-ranked me on this one, - *setting up a happy family unit*.

Now don't get irritated. I am happy for you, and don't forget me coming all the way for your marriage, we all had such a blast. I was on crutches yet I managed to dance on my one leg. My dad was as bemused as ever with me, and wanted to disown me as always.

You can imagine my state, I am now dependent on Kuber sending me the dollars to be able to complete my masters degree, for dad has refused to finance me.

I made the mistake of my life coming back to India and trying out the F&B business. I had to leave the country broke, and listen to rebukes all over again from Dad. Sad luck. Yug was a gem, he took the loss on his chin.

Our partnership did not work out. I hope yours does. Do be careful of Kuber, he is too shrewd and apt at spreading false rumours.

It is sad, that whenever I am in India you are away.

Now I hear from Kuber you are returning back and hope to collaborate with him, over some offshore tech business in India. Now I am away.

I am sure you have all the hot shot connections in London. But will your children like it in India? That too after their propah'English schools. Oh blimey!

I don't intend to spread mistrust, but just warn you about Kuber. He says all kinds of things to me about you. Yet he has helped me immensely. He has been with my father in business after I left, and I am told money was mismanaged on site.

Kuber also tells me Dad owes him money. I am not sure whether Dad could be the best mentor to Kuber, I thought they were so alike and they would get along. I don't know whom to trust!

Sarkaar tells me I have done the most foolish thing in my life, so I am warning you about Kuber, who I thought was my only friend in America. I hope Dad does not ruin it for me.

Yug visited me in Texas, and went back and told people in India that I am depressed. I just like dark grey and used that as the base paint in my large home.

I live alone in a four bed house, with a huge lawn. There is peace and a bit too much of quiet.

The music collection we set up in college days is in one room, the cassettes and CD's more of a relic now. I have a study desk in another, on which I sit and brood.

The fourth room is empty for guests, without a bed, and my master bedroom is as large as the attached toilet to it.

Yug perhaps coming from Bombay could not adjust to the idea of space, after all he lives in a typical Bombay house himself. Yet he is so happy and full of energy and always up to something. Such a foolish eternal optimist! I wish we were like him.

More till I hear from you, my struggling University days of working at mcDonalds are over, but I hope I land up a good job after the MBA program.

It's tough at thirty plus, and I have to return Kuber's money too.

Wish me some of your proverbial good luck.

Hope to see you in India when I travel there next.

It will be Dad's seventy fifth, and though he will never accept it, I will do the best I can to throw the best possible bash for him.

He's not been the best dad in town, but I still hope he can see in me, the best son.

Chalo Sid, Bye ;-) P

15. A Simile and Metaphor
A figure of speech based on resemblance and similarity.

Illustration:
They can go together. Just like friends.

(Simile) He lies like an auctioneer.
(Metaphor) With a smooth, albeit a fork shaped tongue, he spoke.

15. Sarkaar's Diary

Hello Diary,

I have observed with the passage of time, the deteriorating nature of our past alliance what we could have called friendship – has all turned bogus.

No one really cares about my opinion, so here is my own narrative.

A record of events for myself, lest I forget in old age.

It will help me to remember, incase I make the mistake that Sid is making; to trust is to falter at the feet of others.

Our friends are not our pals. They are merely people who surround us at a time in our life, when we fail to choose correctly. Then, they keep re-appearing.

I tried all my life, from those school day incidents. To forgive and forget. To overcome everything they did, my so-called friends.

There was the thing with Kuber, he was a man in a hurry, going nowhere. He created interesting situations though, not being frank or truthful, rather being manipulative and lying his way through trouble- knowing the way of the world.

People around him were not interested in him, rather they were self-interested too. As long as he could serve their purpose and get them what they wanted, they would tolerate him, or keep him in their list of well wishers and friends.

I too used him once or twice, but it was after he visited my home. In our school days, he would make endearing comments with my mother, about our school lunch breaks. I did not misinterpret his sweet words and suspect his intention, as I could see the sparkle in my mother's eyes; she loved the fact, that a friend loved me. Those were simple times.

My mother always worried for my future, and thought I had very few friends. Kuber helped me play a few days in the gymkhana with him. Later even for my daughter to swim we would go together. He gave me some good memories.

I did not hesitate to use his help, these were small things. He had his connection with his club, as I had seen him use Prahlad and Sid unabashedly, to unleash his own plans.

A man who used help as a stepping stone, could bail me out too once in a while. At least that is what I thought.

It was a friendship created out of his own needs.

Kuber never believed in deeds.

Kuber made sure, he would use his access to the club, or use his father's money, his car, his status, to get things done for his friends. Enticing them, doing small material things for them, to make them feel indebted to him.

Was there ever a genuineness in the friendship for the time spent together? We were going for school picnics, playing games, or watching movies in college life – all of it is now feels like a set up or selfish opportunism. A way of I scratch your back, but I will not allow you to scratch my back, unless I want it scratched.

It feels like so long back.

What hurt most, is these pals, these friends, not bothering to call me, when I lost my wife, my life partner. The only person I could speak to was Sid. I cried my heart out over the video calls to him, and he took it.

Sid took my calls repeatedly. I already knew he was genuine, because he was always like that.

The rest made no effort. They called it space.
Space they were giving me.
Me and my grief, being given space.
Space my arse.

They are basically selfish and busy in their own lives.
They did not even try.

In death, one remains alone to suffer the absence of the loved one.

When my friends die, I realize I will be more shaken than them. If I were to go first, it won't matter. My life does not matter to them. I learnt that the hard way. Either way, one has to get over death of another.

One cannot go together, though I loved my wife, she went early, way too early. Here I am on this planet, left alone. The intensity of the loss, is for the one left behind to bear.

Suddenly, with my wife gone, death has become a reality, up close and personal. It can hit any one of us. Yet, we think we will live forever. We forget the mournful days post our loved ones departure.

Every grave loss, has it's tenure.
So does camaraderie.

I now focus on myself, I must walk, I must keep on walking. I go on long walks, it is the only way to fight depression.

And diabetes. And hypertension.

It heals me.

It makes me feel, mobile and light.

There is a sense of walking away from grief.

Activity. It lightens the loss.

One can be on the planet and bear the drudgery of bereavement and collapse into poor health. Or fight depression and stay back. Live. Live long.

Live a bit for others and also for oneself.
Be stoic and strong to live a long life.

Sid had warned me in school, '*be selfish about your health*' he used to say. I will now take that seriously. One life, yours, live it fully Mr. Som Sarkaar.

For so many years, we were bothered by small stupid incidents of each other's lives, and now in death, there was no show of sorrow. By anyone.

Nothing to make me feel less sad. Even when I lived alone.

Is that what friends are for?

I contemplated suicide. It was common they said. To feel like that.

I loved my self too much they said. I would not be able to take the leap toward death.

They never bothered to call.

Living alone now by myself, is not easy.
At times, a person can imagine dreary things.

I feel ghosts come visiting, knowing you are sad.
They are like crows.
Maybe even my ancestors.

Then one thinks, 'Are you losing your mind? What is all this work stress for in life, if every thing is so impermanent.'

The thing about friendships, is that you get to know so much about each other over a period of time.

The dark little secrets, the actions not taken, the truths spoken, the time spent together, where from your gut, you know how the other will react in certain circumstances.

Some friends share their crushes, some their strong dislikes of even each other, and yet all five of us, had been around each other for over ninety percent of the time of our formative years.

Where were they when you needed them?

Prahlad doing women. Sid making money. Yug taking care of his own family.

Kuber, aargh. I want to tear that guy open. Scratch his eyes out. Fold his ears and box him behind his head.

He made a big hue and cry to invest in his project. Multiple projects. None that I can figure.

They all sounded like sand castles in the air.

That is all he wanted. Serenity Hotels. Land, walls, sand, concrete, cement steel. Goa, Goa, Goa. He's gone. His heart has changed to stone.

We have gone past our own dark events of each others lives, often acting as if the other should not be affected at all.

No affection, no show of love or friendship, even for effect. Complete bogey, this bonhomie.

Kuber thinks of himself as a superior. Actually he has an inferiority complex. Unlike Prahlad – who really has a superiority complex.

Two extremes.

One jealous, living with the fear of missing out. The other narcissistic.

Kuber is the only one, yearning for something else always. He got to a point, always discontent with his current state of affairs. He over-pranked, over extended himself, and yet was never loyal to anyone but himself in the pentagon of our camaraderie.

He ensured, that the rest of the four of us, could never operate without him. He often spread a false lie, between any two of us to the third or fourth person. Rumour mongering, gossiping, lying. All of us fell for it.

Until I caught it, by speaking to his father. And his mother. And Prahlad's father. Neither of their versions added up.

Kuber has noticed that Sid was the one with a strong spine for our friendships keeping us all together. He has broken that spine away.

Prahlad was always self-obsessed, and Yug was busy with his own large family and their personal problems. If at all, he was more attached to Prahlad as one would be to his sweet-heart.

Since now I am back to being single, I can only be looking up to Sid; I mean, I know, I can never get married.

Yet, I never played favourites openly, with or against anyone. They just never could relate to me, or embrace me.

It was just Sid, keeping us together.

The rest, are like any other regular guys, who were not part of a square, as they saw life being more circular, continuous and often, going off tangent from the geometry of design they had in mind.

Yet they would come back into the circle of each other's influence, form a square and often accommodate Kuber into the pentagon, and morph back into a square or a triangle with me, based on which of the set of twos, threes, or four friends were left.

Each of these guys, except Kuber, had at the core of their heart, no agenda, no plan against or for each other. They were happy to listen to music, as much as go aimlessly for a drive.

The mistake we all made, was that we rarely concurred or conferred with each other, about Kuber, and the rumours or message he had spread between us, against each other.

This kept us on the wrong path or wrong track for very long, without the realization that he was neither their enemy, nor their friend. He was simply experimenting with us, testing us, literally toying with us for some sadistic, annoying, cryptic fun, for the sheer joy of it.

That is who Kuber was. A sardonic arsehole.

Disruptive, dangerous and random, for no real reason, other than his own past. Yet how much can you discount the past, when life is hitting us all in the fast lane too.

Sid had his old folks.
Yug had the entire old family.
Prahlad had no one, yet he had to remain on the lookout for a wife.

Sadly, Prahlad took my situation similar to his own.

Well, it is clearly not the same thing, but that is Prahlad's intelligence, or the lack of applicability of it. He never had a wife. I had lost mine.

So now we both were without a wife.

Logically he was right. Except that I had the experience of the past to carry, and he just carried the expectant future.

Amongst the five of us, each one had at some time or the other stood up, and bailed one or the other out of a sticky situation.

Like Sid in college days, was neither rich nor over wealthy. Yet he always made me comfortable.

Yug never crossed anyone's path, or harmed anyone either, he was safe rather than sorry. Yet he clung on to Prahlad from school days.

He was originally more fond of Kuber, but could see the change in the man, before any of us. He mistakingly with Sid, made Prahlad apologize to Kuber, for nothing at all.

It was all due to Prahlad's father's decisions, that Kuber never agreed upon and the business split, causing the friends to feel the pinch.

At some level, it made Yug into a loner. He clung to his office friends.

Like Prahlad. He always emulated Prahlad, and perhaps thought that was a safe haven to be in.

He had suffered a small business loss with Prahlad earlier in the F&B space more stoically. The break with Kuber, that broke us all apart – was more devastating to Yug, than to any one of us.

Perhaps he too was going through so much, like me. He kept a safe distance.

Sensible.

That's what I think of Yug Ikani. A great friend maybe not to me, yet, he never relied on others for help.

Prahlad Ahuja, oh he changed once he left for America.

Each time he came to India, he was looking for a bride, who could live and adjust with him in America.

Each time he was in America, he wanted to come to India, and each time he was in India, he just felt like flying back to America.

That is Prahlad for you.
A friend?
Nah...

Lost in transit. Yeah!

Migration had taken a toll on his rationality, and he kept kneeling before material progress, over emotional bonds.

Yet he yearned for closeness with his family, who did nothing for him. They hurt him, yet he did not hurt them back, nor his friends ever.

This turned his life into a placid, boring version of his pompous life from school days. He had all his desires taken care of.

He never knew his need.

Despite always being a front ranker in college, he felt he lagged behind each of us, for the late marital dalliance he got himself in and out of in America.

He married a western girl, to have a family and breed kids, and his first wife left him for a generous alimony. Prahlad almost immediately re-married on the re-bound. He was conspicuous in his own absence.

Other than on landmark dates, when he called to wish me on my birthday, I can't say much more about him, that I understood.

I felt reciprocating on his. I felt like telling him, to wish his own narcissistic self. But I did not, as everyone in his own family had been so bad to him, that it felt like a mean thing to do.

That's not what friends are for.

Prahlad did make the effort to show me around Europe, at a time when I was behaving like a miser, he picked all my bills, and we both travelled to see Europe.

This led to alleviating his pain in trying to reduce mine. But I could make no conversations, no heart to heart with him. His emotions had been snuffed out. By his past.

He started every day and looked at the future, through the prism of past events, failing to change or adapt his life.

He landed at every moment, every today, disconnected and unhappy.

He was missing his love partner, but exactly who was that?

Yet, the great thing about Prahlad Ahuja - he let's you be. He let's himself be too. Unlike Kuber, he does not disrupt or disrespect you. He is a great travel partner a sweet host. He got me pillows at night from house keeping. He also lives well.

Kuber came from a family, that was neither broken, nor strong, where the bonds were commercial and money meant everything.

Kuber's sister had been married off twice, and past two broken relationships was suffering schizophrenia – battling it in the family. That's what Kuber told us. Yet he did not know, he suffered the same way. Their deeds created their destiny.

They blamed it on luck. On others.

Kuber had eventually married Rekha out of guilt rather than love. His own marriage had been one of convenience. He ended up using his wife, who became an American citizen.

He freely lived off her, her job and her money. He eventually divorced her, taking more than half their assets and swelling his own bank balances.

Well, he learnt well in America, acting for alimony; what a friend indeed! Both Rekha and Prahlad, suffered the same consequences.

Choosing wrong partners.

A friendship in many ways is a marriage of minds, and souls – not very unlike a marriage, with no prenup or divorce options.

It is just not a union of bodies.

Friendship is relieved of the responsibilities and shitty parts that are difficult and require heavy lifting in a marriage.

If you cannot be a good friend, can you manage a marital relationship? I wish I could muster the courage to ask both Prahlad and Kuber the same question.

I pray, Prahlad will do better, on all counts. He is a better human for sure. But their family foundations are both weak.

In a friendship filled with bonhomie, you simply take off from where you left years ago. It is like landing and taking off in an aeroplane at and from exactly the same spot.

Well, Kuber would say, '*Why all this Philosophy Phucker!*' Little did we know then back in school, he was the one who was the fuc&#@er!

He lacked the clarity of mind, and the magnanimity of the heart.

Bonhomie is usually built on the foundation of a past, or a circumstance where someone has bailed you out. Stood by you and still had made light of the situation. A spirit, when you are with people, that relaxes you and not pressurizes or depletes you.

The senses play the same role in love at first sight.

You simply get along from the moment go. The advantage with such friendships is that you do not have to cope with them as you do with family members.

You accept your friends for what they are, and you know their shortcomings, but you do not seek a change, nor do you avoid frankness. You can tell them what you wish, unlike your family.

This works, till your friends become like family.

Sid came into contact with them again in college life, when he, Prahlad and Kuber signed up for their Architecture pre-exams tutorials with the same math teacher.

Everyone enjoyed the light hearted tomfoolery that Kuber was good at, and kept everyone in high spirits. The math teacher would use Sid's disposition and Prahlad's seriousness to go deep into studies that everyone including Kuber emulated.

This grouping was devoid of me and Yug, both using our self study time and managing within the framework of family frugality, mixed with tenacity.

Yug and I are self-taught. We came up the hard way and got to the same place as the other three, at no extra costs to our families.

This was when Architecture college fees in India for the entire five years, was less than a thousand dollars and tutorials were barely a couple of hundred dollars.

Talking about money, Kuber always wanted to earn a fast buck. Prahlad though entrenched in self importance, never broke rules. He always warned Sid, that Kuber rarely followed rules.

Kuber always broke rules. Law, was meant to be broken. He helped people in other devious ways, and made their lives, like Rekha's. Cheating in examinations as in life.

Kuber rarely respected meritocracy, and devised ways to break the queue and jump ahead. If the means justified the end, it was a happy end for him.

Yug was always accepting of everyone. Sid and Prahlad found this odd, but did nothing to correct him, or disassociate themselves from Kuber when they were young, until that unfortunate night on the eve of each of them flying off to America.

Infact, Prahlad sought Kuber's help to finance his own higher studies, and Kuber got stuck in a trap – with his father's

business as compensation – one that he never got.
Talk about double standards, and I scratch your back...

This just led to so much bad blood, over the previously spilled school blood bath mixed with spilt milk and spilled beans.

Rumours destroyed whatever lies the friendships hinged on.

When truth appears like lies, and lies become the real narrative, no one knows what to believe. Friendship does not thrive in such unreal chaos.

Kuber and Sid's friendship was struck when Sid was visiting India. They would meet for dinner with Yug and his wife or just by themselves. Rekha never joined them, even when she was in India.

Simi always did.

It had become an odd grouping.

There was no time to make assessments about people's nature. Sid also inherently always trusted everyone, and never had any dislike toward anyone as a person.

Sid was always there for them in calamity and always able to fund their needs with breaking up his own pocket money or earnings with them as a young kid.

Sid never ran out of time, or money. It was as if both were at his will and command, available like him to his friends.

There was no other person more loved in his colony than Sid. I certify that.

After graduation, all of them got into jobs, and married their spouses...as time and age passed.

So did my wife.

Yug did exceedingly well in his career and rose to the ranks of becoming a Vice President in his company. Kuber decided to go into his Goa Hotel business and Prahlad migrated overseas for his MBA, saying goodbye and 'I told you so, I was the most intelligent.'

Prahlad did not pay back the debt to Kuber.
That is what Kuber claimed.
Prahlad's father cheated Kuber too.
That was what Kuber told Sid.
It was a double whammy for Kuber.

No one knew what the truth was.

None of us suspected that Kuber did any wrong. He was a charmer, so Sid fell for it, as had Yug.

Kuber decided to become hard, and learnt to take deceit in his stride. But he never forgot that Prahlad did not bail him out, even later once they both made money.

The thing was that Prahlad was suffering the loss of alimony as much as I was suffering the loss of my wife.

I did tell Yug to intervene then. Yet Yug never listened to my advice. The first crack in our friendship was thus rekindled again.

Alas, the bonhomie was now completely dead.

'**Was**'...is what Kuber muttered under his breath. 'By the time you comeback, I **will** be making more money with my Mumbai and Goa hotels, than what your father had ever made.' He had said this to Prahlad.

He had vowed this before me at the airport, when we all went to wish Prahlad good bye. Their lives were not stable, and they were yet to settle in marriage at the ripe age of 35.

A year later from that Airport departure of Prahlad, Sid decided to follow suit and move out of Bombay for a job in London. It finally broke up the group of college friends, and each one had to go their own way.

(The above transcript of Som Sarkaar's dialogue to himself in his dairy, was posted by snail mail to Yug in India. Sarkaar had made a copy from Russia, where he was posted with GCS on a large Oil and Gas station project. He had hoped that Yug would corroborate and understand better, urging him to repair things.)

Ψ

Yug on the phone, 'Sarkaar, my man, very in depth thoughts on record. That too in writing. Your thoughts, can lead to action. A lot of fighting action. Give me some time to think.'

Sarkaar replies, 'Do you feel I have been true to us, the Pentagon of Bonhomie?' The words reach Yug, with some lag and echo.

The words repeat in Yug's earlobe and his sleepy conscience. 'Intense man, very intense,' is all he can come up with.

Sarkaar was keen to know Yug's opinion on his diary notes. His internal dialogue with himself, had nudged him to a point where he wanted to mend things.

'Well, I don't know, the lesser said the better,' Yug enlarges his eyeballs, as his wife Diya is waiting for dinner.

Having had a cataract operation, his multifocal lenses had not improved his vision on bonhomie.

'Still...' wanting to evoke a response, Sarkaar prods on.

'You know me Sarkaar. I have always kept to myself, and I speak the least out of the lot. I also have put the least time from my side in this association. I do know, I missed out on warning Kuber and protecting him from Prahlad's father, but that was what Prahlad should have done.'

'That is why your opinion matters the most. We could save Sid the same trouble that Kuber and Prahlad have been through.'

There is silence.

Sarkaar continues, 'We must save Sid from Kuber.'

Yug replies, 'Everyone knows how Kuber is since our school days. Why will Sid listen to me? Frankly, they both left me out of things, when they got into arrangements with Kuber. Let Sid now bear the brunt of it, if he has not learnt from Prahlad's experience. '

'Exactly, you only care about Prahlad,' blames a slightly agitated Som Sarkaar.

'That's not true, but that is what you all feel. Yes, during the loss you faced at your wife's demise, we should have been there, but there was so much going on here.' Yug waits for a few seconds.

'Look Yug, if we do not intervene and warn Sid, he could be in trouble. Prahlad has fore warned you about it.' A concerned Sarkaar speaks into the phone.

Yug retorts, 'Sid will take the advice from you. Not from me or Prahlad.'

'It is his life. His choice. I will do what I can to help both Simi and Sid, if they were to decide to eventually come back to India. Let me wait till he approaches me about it. Sid had approached me to check on the winery business in India, but I was myself not interested, to move away from the Software and Architecture design space. There is no expertise either of us have in wineries.'

Som Sarkaar makes the final attempt, 'Look at it this way, some day, each of us will be eighty years old, with no one to sit with together. If we retain the bonhomie, we will be together maybe going to Goa for a holiday, despite the petty issues.'

'Let me see what I can do. I will talk to you again, now don't worry so much.' Yug disconnects the call, and himself from the issue, saying his goodbye to Sarkaar.

Diya asks him, 'So Mr. Yug Ikani, your Pentagon is more important than our routine dinner?'

'I dunno' about that. Sid does not easily listen to me. I made the mistake of making Prahlad apologize to Kuber. Now if I meddle with Sid, Kuber could get upset with me. The last thing I need, is Kuber Savla on my tail.'

'So what will you do?' asks Diya, as she passes Yug the '*alooTook.*'

'Let Sid cope with it. He will manage. It is me who has high blood pressure, so let us stay away from this *jing-bang bhel puri* being made in Mumbai.'

'Let us think of ourselves, that's the way to save oneself. That is what Prahlad did, and that is what Kuber is going to do. Sid is collateral damage, which is self-inflicted if he is foolish enough to follow Kuber's line of thinking.'

'Well, that's not what friends are for,' warns Diya.

Yug, responds with his hands and mouthful, 'Well, a friend in deed, is a friend indeed, and Sid is an unstoppable machine for that. Almost a human robot as a problem solver. It is his time to return to India, and he will fall for it, hook line and sinker.'

16. Climax

A figure of speech, in which an arrangement of ideas is done in order of increasing importance.

Illustration:
Humble in nature, noble in behaviour, zealous in action, strong in character. My friend indeed.

16. Kuber : In transit

'Real life is so strange Sid, who would have thought, I would see you here at Heathrow, in transit.' Kuber dumps his bags at the back of Sid's Audi Q7.

'Well, here you are.' Sid smiles to himself, more than toward Kuber.

As they drive, they talk about their old times, their Matheran picnic has them in splits. Kuber's face hardens a bit, but Sid misses that while watching the traffic.

Kuber talks about his relationship changes and souring of his marriage with Rekha openly, and the lack of children and the freedom it gives him to take risks.

Sid spots the London Museum, as he turns toward Camden.

He listens quietly as it takes him time to absorb. Mentally he tells himself, '*Kuber, and wealth. Really the God of wealth this guy seems to think he is. Monstrous in one way, repulsive looking with his hard features and toad like eyes. Yet charismatic with his imperfections, a useful deformity.*'

Leathery skinned and darker than usual, Kuber has thinned out further after college life. He appears to have lost all sex appeal – looking part man, having part woman like mannerisms.

Sid remembers the eunuchs in India, and a very strange feeling comes across his mind; he shudders. '*Why really did I agree to meet Kuber?*' He wonders.

'Thanks for picking me up, I did not know I could count on you Sid. Initially I thought it was a stop over at the airport, but the connecting flight has got delayed for over a day and a half. Thanks pal,' says Kuber.

He breaks Sid's trail of thoughts and gets him back from the traffic light begging eunuchs in India he had seen on his last holiday.

'Any time.' Sid comes across as false as he feels, and he knows it, that Kuber knows it.

Thinking to himself, Sid silently drives, '*Like any other college association you do it for the spirit of bonhomie you enjoyed then, knowing fully well the different kind of highways your lives have traversed, and exit routes taken. This too will die its timely death.*'

Sid comments to break the tranquility setting in the car, 'This one goes back to school times pal, you were something then. Simi was always curious about all of us, how we hung around through thick and thin.'

'Hmm, hmm,' mumbles Kuber, dissatisfied internally, thinking of the lovely Simi marrying Sid. 'These residences look regal and quaint at the same time,' he says to Sid. 'Lucky bastard!' he mutters under his breath, thinking of Simi's vivaciousness, perhaps it has kept Sid's youth and libido intact.

Sid smiles, 'Yes, the British have built their homes well.'

'I wish we can build a hotel of this kind some day. Goa. The land is there, the spot is there close to the beach,' dreams Kuber.

'We? You mean you. What is stopping you?' asks a surprised Sid, he has tried several times to stay away from ventures of the kind Kuber keeps proposing.

'Sister's situation, she is dependent upon me and Rekha cannot bear the load anymore. She has been the only one with a stable income. Now Rekha too has raised her hands, my folks just don't understand.'

The car stops at a red light. There has never been closeness with Kuber, but Sid's young life has always been spent showing Kuber his mistakes, trying to put him on the right path.

'Your mother has always been so concerned for you, sheer and pure love. Rekha has been industrious and loyal to you. What more do you want?' Sid asks in a nonplussed sort of way.

Kuber acting in jest, speaks his heart out, 'Love from the wife and loyalty from the mother – the other way round would have been better. Is it not?'

Sid tries to show the bigger picture, 'See, we are encircling the entire block, to reach our residence, it is the way the roads are planned to avoid congestion.'

'Not everyone is lucky like you,' responds Kuber.

'Well, one has to work hard on relationships, it takes away a lot of time.' Sid continues to smile, showing an external disposition that is cool, while boiling on the inside.

Kuber throws a spanner in the works, 'Yug says your own sister has always been needy, sought your help and never showed up to support you in your life. How have you handled that?'

Sid clarifies, 'Is that Yug, or your assessment based on meeting my mum in India? That is the way life is. You cannot do anything with others expectations. As long as they think I am capable it is okay.'

The all knowing Kuber, interjects 'Oh I know everything from Prahlad and Yug. They have shared with me. The least your sister could have done, is provided you with the emotional support, to return to India at some point. In the end, money is thicker than blood. Yes, your own mum has only confirmed that about your sister.'

Sid tries, 'The saying goes, blood is thicker than...' he recollects that Kuber and his sister have the same sun sign, the same birth date.

Kuber cuts him off, 'Yeah yeah, I know, it's just about money these days.'

Sid goes into a sullen mood, withdraws, and appears pensive, thinking about his own family back home.

The manipulative Kuber continues, 'So, let's visit the London Eye, their giant wheel in the evening, I have never been here.'

'Hmm..,' trails of Sid.

Not one to give space, Kuber shoots from the hip, 'So how is Simi?' in afterthought, 'And the kids?'

'Well, a spread that is not worthy of you, awaits you at home. Rest, shower and we will step out as soon as you are ready before the evening sunset. You can take back photographs in that area, sights of bridges over the river Thames, the half drawn Tower bridge and dear ol'Big Ben at the eastern end of parliament.'

Later at home, Kuber casts a wider net, 'Simi, your husband has gone all cold after his sister's controversy and proverbial needs from him. You cannot just sit so relaxed and not take a little bit of risk. India is in a boom stage, and now is the time if any, to return.'

Sid is unable to talk any detail, about the past of their friendship and the reasons he has never entangled himself in any India business with Kuber.

He tries to gesticulate to Simi, to avoid getting into Kuber's trap, but the comment strikes a chord with Simi.

'I have been after him since years. This is not our land, not our city, not our country. We live like foreigners here.'

'Well, Yug never has the guts for a venture, however curious he is about it. He repeatedly misses out. Prahlad would make a great partner, but once into anything, he develops cold feet. I expected Sid to be the champion right from school days he has been the boss of the school and our gang! Born to be boss like Bruce Springsteen.'

'Born in Bombaaaay....' trails Sid in the same tune like Boss' song. 'What will I do in Goa? I am not from the hospitality sector, and handling organized labour is not my cup of tea. We will never be able to leave Bombay once I retire.'

Kuber springs another attempt, 'Look, each of us, has done the best we can for our families, sisters and even their families. It is time, that we live a little bit for ourselves.'

'My work here will take time to settle and,...' Sid leaves the sentence unfinished, and Kuber takes over from where he left off earlier.

'Run the Mumbai office for me, while I shuttle, between Mumbai and Goa. Imagine the pleasant sun-sets and weather in December, January. You will think you are in England as half of our tourists come from here for a holiday. Ten months in Mumbai and two in Goa, the right balance.'

'Why live this glum life? I always dreamt of being in Goa. Let us give Kuber's venture a shot,' over commits a zealous Simi.

Kuber uses the opening to build it up in Sid's head, 'Sid is the proverbial friend to us all. Humble in nature, noble in behaviour, zealous in action, strong in character. My friend indeed.'

Simi has only fond memories of her serenading days with Sid in old Bombay. When Rekha too would join in the joint dates together for movies, walks at Marine Drive and shopping at Pedder Road, ending with a musical night at Jazz by the bay.

Over strawberries dipped in chocolate sauce at Borough's Market, Simi displays her over familiarity and is overjoyed that Kuber's visit has served as an opportunity to return to India. 'Sid can put in his papers and join you by the end of the year. Our kids are doing well. Both are in Edinburgh and don't seem to be keen to return back.'

'True that, we are done with our responsibilities...' Sid thinks aloud.

Simi suggests and reminds Sid, 'You are the one, who used to say, a friend in deed, is a friend indeed. Now's the time to show it.'

Kuber has cast his net wide for a big catch, with even Simi batting for him.

'How much can you wait on children? You are done with here, and it fits both our objectives. I am that friend in need...' fills in Kuber.

Sid catches his hand and silences him with a handshake.

Before Sid knows it, Kuber has manipulated the situation so well, that Simi is already over excited to be there.

Little does she know, that there is trouble brewing for Sid ahead.

Too much trouble.

17. Allusion

A figure of speech, referring to another fable or famous story. A writer's short-cut.

Illustration:
Her hospital visits were your medication.

She got your pole climbing like Jack and the bean stalk.

17. The Reply

Dear P,

Shorthand bugger, Mr. Prahlad ! When will you ever settle down? And where?

We hope you have a good life. Saw the date and realized I had missed your birthday, so belated wishes and sorry man. I forgot. Plain and simple. Time surely flies.

My apologies again that I took so long to reply and talk to you. As you know, I always do get back, albeit my reply having come after so much time, that I pray it has changed your situation.

Sad to disappoint you again- but all Simran's cousins are mums already with many of them out of shape and out of reckoning.

So don't keep using your intelligence alone, use your heart. Let it lead the brain, you nerd! Else who and how and when will you ever find yourself a partner. Then you say, you are lagging behind, but you led all along in school and in your Casanova life. It looked rocking on the outside, but your lil'P(eter) must be tired on the inside;-)) Take a break pal.

I am sure you have given so much lovin' and must be tired too of the drilling. Ahem ahem.

Broken more than your share of a few hearts? It is coming back to bite you now. Think, and act, as your deeds will catch up with your actions my friend.

Commit to the right girl for yourself and for her, especially if she is head over heels in love. I know I know, you will say I judge you, etc. Yet, that is the only way you can have a life, which has any semblance with mine.

Else don't compare. Marriage comes with it's share of sacrifices and perhaps you are not willing to make them.

I believe you have changed very little after going to America.

If at all, you have become narcissistic. That is hardly a change for the better. You asked for honest brutal feedback over the phone, of what friends think, so here goes.

Ideally, don't get married. Period.

Yet, if you have to ('coz you will not take a friend's advice) I would rather you get entangled with an unknown American girl's life. She will teach you more than an Indian would tolerate from you.

I believe the Americans don't stay married forever, and you will still have a good run for a decade. Rather than an Indian girl, not that I know any directly besides Simi's connections.

No one will want to leave India and join you. I also know you pal. They will not be able to adjust in *your* America.

It is not as if Indian girls are easy, if they are still unmarried, they will either have emotional baggage, or some issue in their own family that still keeps them unmarried in India. They will not be keen to settle abroad. Unless you are looking at someone over a decade younger than you. And why would such a young woman marry you? Oh, your money!!

Sorry pal, sorry, but you asked me to be frank with you, so here I am, threadbare, your friend writing to you as bluntly as possible.

On another front, think of returning. To India. Maybe that works better for your life. Lets look at it differently.

India is in a good space, if you can take the noise, din with pollution all year round. We moved here start of this year, and have found a permanent domestic help. I know you had warned via Yug too, and in your earlier correspondence, but Kuber has made me invest in his venture.

He says he had loaned money to your father, so his funds are stuck in your dad's company. I don't know why he does not ask you the relevant questions, but he keeps hissing and dissing about your dad.

Look into it with your father.

Perhaps you should shift to NY or Miami and live it up for a while. Brighten up things away from Kansas. I am not the best to give American advice, never travelled across the Atlantic like you blokes.

It is not just luck, but sheer hard work to raise two kids too.
Ask Yug, he stopped after one.

So while you credit me for a happy life, and you say that you are happy for me, it has taken many sacrifices. Many more from Simi. Not easy to find a life partner like her, who is a great mom too.

As you asked for a written letter, I have made the effort, so please please do not feel lonely and stop having these anti-depressants.

Yes, I will be there for your dad's bash.

You sure were a good son, but watch out getting hurt and sandwiched between him and y/our buddy Kuber.

Money always breaks friendships.

I know you have warned me often, but Simi is hooked into the belief that we are on a money spinner with the Goan life. So I will have to be ok to lose money, and the friendship of Kuber, if it goes south.

He claims there's nothing else but opportunity for both of us.

I know Kuber as much as you do, he is only after creating wealth for himself, and has had some rough times, so I feel sorry for him. (Two para's starting with I know,...I am beginning to sound like you!)

Rekha till now was busy with her own family, so Kuber keeps complaining that his relationship has soured. He also lives off her earnings, as she is the one bringing in the stable income, so they were together. Now both have gone their separate ways.

Ultimately that's how marriages run, it is an economic and an emotional dalliance.

At times you think it the other way round with us men too, it is the same. So perhaps Kuber is the one wearing the skirts in his marriage. He needs help, and finally with all things sorted financially for my sister too, I am doing what I can to support him.

Perhaps it will change his fortunes if not his nature.

If it does not work, hopefully it will help him feel secure, that besides his own sister, and any other person, a friend loves him.

I sense Kuber feels very unloved, despite being married to Rekha; who in the past appeared to have been head over heels in love with him. I don't know what went wrong. Why things became faint and why their affections reduced with age?

It should be the other way round.

I am accompanying him to Goa, as he wants me to look at a parcel of land. We have viewed Karjat and found it very unlike the cosmopolitan place we are in search for.

More him. I am just drifting along so that he has a second opinion or view that he claims he seeks.

More when we meet. So don't worry, be happy! (listen to music pal)

Bye,
Sid.
Sidey days are here again. Goaaaaaah !
2nd December 2013.

P.S.: I will be happy if you find love again. Find an Indian girl, she will do you justice. Always give love a chance. Do come back to India, I am sure you will find her, here only.

So on second thoughts, leave the Americans alone. Let them be depressed, it is time you move on.

Ψ

Yug's letter to Prahlad
22nd Feb '2014
Yug Ikani
Bombay 52. India

Dear Prahlad,

Years have passed.

It appears as if our friendship lies in the debris of the Gulf war, which also got over couple of years ago. Our friendship has now outlasted the war.

To me, ideologically, there seems to be no commonality left, as is the case with India and USA.

We have our own elections brewing here, and the rife corruption in India gives so much hopelessness to our folks watching television.

Perhaps your father has not much to look forward to.

Since you really haven't found a partner there, why don't you consider the troupe of girls whom you took out for dancing in our last Goa trip with Sid?

We thought we were making our bachelor trip after your Dad's party, but you seem to have turned on your charm. Ahem, ahem...

Is there hope in getting in touch with Sagarika from that Goa trip? Think it through, our children are entering high school, and you don't seem to have got started yet.

I still recollect Sid's convalescence and your hospitalization in Goa. Man, oh Man, eating food with a lizard cooked in it, only Sid could have survived that, as if nothing hit him. That man has some luck and health. God is always with him.

We both nearly died in the hospital.

I guess God heard his prayers for us.

You would remember the food poisoning and the aftermath of trips to and fro that Sagarika made. Her hospital visits were your medication. She got your pole climbing like Jack on the bean stalk. Ahem, ahem.

She is in Mumbai these days. And forget about the fact that your sister thinks she was after the family wealth. The pace at which you and your dad seem to be losing wealth, nothing much will really remain for any girl to consider running away with.

Either way, you have to create your own life pal, and every girl looks for some security. Didn't each of you friends sisters?

Sid remembers the girl too.

He feels she is not suited for you. He fears, that you fear separations more than looking forward to unions. He thinks she is too passionate for you to handle;-);-) and does not want to dissuade or encourage you.

Perhaps you worry too much about dealing with your own family devils and the past. You will only find out if you give it a shot.

I and Sid seem to agree on one thing though, always give love a chance, perhaps you have not found it, as you keep seeking it.

Let me remind you my almighty, we are all ageing and mere mortals. So remember you are from the same batch as us.

You gotta make the first move my friend. Wait no more...Sid has assured me, he will act as your best man, and gladly give you away, tired as we all are, taking emotional care of you.

Take care buddy, we can't stop worrying for you,

Yug

India. 2014/2/22

BTW: there seems to be a right wing leader appointed and approved by the RSS in India to lead the opposition party to power.

If they win in the corrupt mood created by the current dispensation, it will be the first time, that India will get a proven Chief Minister to run India. If they win...if you return...

Well someone has to create history in India...inspiration for you to return?

P.S.: India...India... like the chants in the cricket stadiums.

Show some loyalty and patriotism.

~Yug

18. Understatement

A Figure of speech – that makes a simple sentence look less serious, bad or negative, a sort of Bogey trap for the target, set by the trap setter, to put the person off-balance or off guard.

Illustration:
'I make you an offer, you can't refuse.'

18. You cannot refuse

Simi is a bit upset, but she lets it show more than normal.

'You did not have to go to Goa alone.' She appears moody and miffed. That is a dangerous combination for any husband. 'I have given you enough latitude. Why did it have to be Goa without us? The kids would have loved it too.'

'I am not going alone, three of us friends are on, it is also a business cum vacay trip.' Sid is peaceful and serene, as he ties a knot, tying up his *cravate and his evening into knots.*

'I always wanted to go with my friends, just the three of us, like the three of you and you always said, two's company, three's a crowd.' Simi sits down glum like a plum.

'That is when two of us, would get together with a solo third friend, not when...' he trails off. 'You are taking my trip!'

'Yes Mr. Siddharth Bhandari, when are you taking us on a trip? You always looking out for friends, you owe me big, and you owe me in Goa.' Simi *prunes her dark plum* mood.

'*Let me make you an offer, **you cannot refuse**.*' Sid appeals. Simi just bats her eyelashes, waiting expectantly acting the dutiful wife.

Simi takes over the conversation as an able wife would, 'After a few years, we will make two trips. One just you and me, and one, just me and my friends, without you. That one will be in Bangkok.'

'I thought I was to make the offer, but I agree. So I pay double, for this one trip,' rues Sid.

'You better will, as always, won't you?' asks Simi.

'Yes Mrs. Bhandari, I will. Now take care of the kids dinner, before you hold me back any further. I have to go and pick *your friend* Rupali, come back to pick you up, and head for Dinshaw's fiftieth on time. He is sending me texts non-stop that he will not cut the cake on his birthday party. If we miss it, and delay any further I will be roasted by him.'

'You can't miss his toast, but you can't be toasted by me. Wow! What loyalty, what friendship.' Simi continues with sarcasm.

'You were my best friend, till we got married.' Sid bites his tongue the moment he blurts out his boy-friend moment of truth.

'I will kill you a second time for that. I am still your best friend.' Simi shouts angrily from the kitchen.

'How many times can I die? Let me live fully once, more profitable for you. I earn more, and...' he can see her stand at the door-frame.

'Am I your best friend or not?' Simi enjoys prolonging any discussion so that she can get a few fleeting private moments with Sid.

Sid romantically, 'Yes my love, you are; it is a matter of love and lust with you – like poetry. He's my best pal. Male pal. Male bond. I mean, Scout's honour, we know each other since...like forty years. It is like a musical band bonhomie.'

Simi continues to spar, 'I know, I know, I am just taking your trip. I told you before, don't get so serious.'

'It would be easier, if you would have joined me on this one, with your three friends.' Sid repartees. 'Kuber has made me an offer, ***you cannot refuse.***'

'Thanks, but no thanks.' That ends it for Simi.

Sid cajoles again, as any tactful, delayed party goer husband would, 'Put on your make up, I will be back at the lobby in ten minutes, and Rupali will be seated ahead, so please just take the back seat.'

'Yes Sid, I am used to that, even with your friends wives.' Simi rocks the boat again with both the oars in her hands.

'Cmon now, she is your best friend in the wives, she is always your drinks partner.' Sid picks up the car keys and heads toward the home exit.

'True that, my Sangria partner.' Simi finally smiles.

'What to do, Capt. Kriplani keeps flying out of the country.' shrugs Sid on his way out. 'Only God knows when we can get together as couples on another Goa holiday. Time is just slipping by...the 50th birthdays have started.'

Simi hangs by the main door of the house, 'Yeah, Rupali sure misses him too. Isn't his birthday next?'

'Nope, he was in France with Rupali last year. Bye now get ready, I will see you in ten. I know you will not miss me. After tonite. It is just a week in Goa for me and time will fly.' Sid runs down the steps of his apartment block.

Sid is back in twelve minutes. Simi is looking fab in her evening black gown, waiting at the lobby. Rupali as expected is seated upfront, and gets down very sweetly, to accommodate Simi. Simi takes her seat in the front seat with her husband, looks at him sarcastically, as Sid drives them both to Dinshaw's birthday.

As they enter, Dinshaw gushes upon hugging Sid, 'Capt Kriplani could not make it,' grumbles Dinshaw. 'He is never around for our special celebrations.'

'What to do? Someone has to earn for a living!' replies Rupali as she walks in. Simi follows her quietly to the bar area. Dinshaw looks at Sid, stupefied.

Sid re-assures, 'It is your birthday DinDin. Enjoy it. Some lesser friends of the past are here. Some good ones are missing, while some who are here, maybe part of your future. You never know. Then there is Capt Sharma. He made sure he did not sail, and he is very much your old boys scout club. Your music band boys are here too. Chin up buddy.'

'Dad has been unwell, his diabetes is troubling him. Mum is not in the mood to shine. Daddy In-Law is here, but unwell with fever. Look at his temperament. He always graces an event, so what if it is for a short while.'

A sudden back-slap hits Sid as he grimaces and turns around, to high-five Mukesh. 'Hey Sidey. I hear you flying back to London tomorrow, do look up Pradeep there.' Mukesh joins the party, embraces Dinshaw and Sid together.

Sid clarifies, 'No man, we are going to Goa, for some work cum pleasure with a set of different friends.'

'Oh here is our opener Mukesh. Batting legend, and bottle opener!' Dinshaw cheers up. 'This guy could open bottle crowns, with his teeth.' Capt Sharma meets with Mukesh with another round of back-slapping, tennis mime hard punches,

'I know, I know. He could hit some good straight drives too.' Capt Sharma comes in with a joint embrace. His wife Anida realizes the boys don't seem to acknowledge her presence.

Anida, 'Chivalry is surely dead!' she breaks off in the direction of Rupali and Simi, and all the ladies congenially get seated together.

The party takes off, with Dinshaw's entire music band boys, the cricket club team, and his childhood buddies, dancing in circles with him. Sid keeps sipping soda and lime cordial, while winking at Dinshaw as he gets himself wasted.

'DinDin, the train's early morning pal,' says Sid, reminding his friend of a bad hangover possible tomorrow.

'Let me live today, tomorrow is another day, who has seen it coming?'

Sid just serenely smiles back. Serenity is on his mind, but of a different kind.

It has to do with the name of a hotels company, that his college friend Kuber Savla wants to start in Goa. After all, it was an offer *he could not refuse*.

19. Rhyme

A speech with rhyme...is not a figure of speech.

19. Journey to Goa

'**H**ey dude, where exactly are we going?' asks Dinshaw.

'We are catching the train buddy, you said you are keen to travel on the Konkan Kanya express. Here we are at C.S.T. station. Wake up!' Exclaims Sid, paying the tea stall vendor.

'He has booked us on first class Dinshaw, what more can we ask for? A train journey to Goa!' Kuber regales with his morning cuppa of tea.

Dinshaw seems perturbed. He hisses, 'I cannot trust this friend of yours Sid. You forget, he always seems to be up to something that turns the scales in his favour. You are too lax with him.'

Sid scratches his moustache. It is a new thick appendage, something he and Simi are not used to. Neither is he, travelling with a different combination of friends.

His is a timid response, 'Let us look forward to the food till Ratnagiri.'

Kuber detects the unwanted feeling that Sid's friend Dinshaw gives him, something he was not aware of before planning the trip.

Kuber had come on to the journey for the purpose to scout land in Goa. Sid was going looking for apartments in Siolim, for his British friends who had heard of a developer doing some solid construction work there.

Sid had also arranged to look for some properties in Panjim city, with the help from one of his British friends who knew the prosperous Sampath family in Goa.

Dinshaw was going because Sid was going, simply to have a good time in Goa. He was happy to just holiday in the resort and look around at Porvorim.

'The compartment and toilets are clean. It really is first class.' said Kuber as he gets into the *bogey, and passes by a few cabins*.

'Well, talk about *a bogey bonhomie on this train full of bogies.*' Dinshaw sizes up the compartment and looks for space to stretch out his legs. 'This long length of wheels and axles will negotiate the Konkan curves well.'

'It is empty!' claims Sid as he sprawls himself over the first class coupe sleeper berth. 'What fun! We used to travel as kids, and go up and down the berth above. Right now, let me try just hoisting myself with my arms...oof! Can't pull my body weight up.'

'I would fear jumping down, and for that I would remain stuck up. You go up and sleep, Mr. Dollar Sai!' Dinshaw, coins a new name for Kuber, hearing about his miserliness throughout the taxi trip. Kuber had been cribbing about the quick changing taxi meter to the two of them on the way to the railway station.

'*Adddey baaabba,* you are going to *Govva*, not Dadar station no?' he would mime an old Sindhi uncle.

Dinshaw had made a grumbling Kuber pay the entire taxi fare. They both laughed their guts out, but the tone was set there.

This new formation of a triangle of friends, was unexpected and unplanned, and it gave Kuber and Sid a new freshness, both feeding off the energy of Dinshaw's jokes and humour, till the train reached Chiplun.

Food vendors carrying sapodilla fruits board their first class compartment. 'They are popularly known as Chickoos, and very good in solving problems related to constipation' Dinshaw tells Kuber.

'They look like your balls to me.' comes Kuber's flat reply. He breaks into peels of laughter on his own joke.

'I will pay for all your food, don't worry, eat pal eat. Come join me.' Dinshaw has already placed food orders with the canteen boy and now picks *chickoos* from the vendor who has come in to sell fruit, water and ice-cream dollies.

He buys a bit of all that is on offer, being charitable and hungry at the same time.

Kuber declines all the three in a huff, and finds the smell of *chickoos* very unpleasant as Dinshaw starts peeling them. He claims, 'I used to share dozens of them with Sid, when my peon used to bring them from his Dhanu farm, why would I eat them now, when I didn't then.'

Sid speaks out of turn to avoid any unpleasantness, 'One can move to Goa for a holiday home, keep it locked through the year, and enjoy the new year eves, beach rave parties and the over all vibe. It is the only place we used to love visiting from London when we would come on our winter holidays.'

Kuber interjects Sid's dreams, 'Let us look for a beach facing parcel of land, it will make good money in the long-term and we can sell it to one of the five star chains. I will take you all to show you the Park Hyatt hotel in South Goa. It is the most iconic property to live in. Why block your money into a small apartment? It is better to own and run a hotel on a piece of land you own.'

Logically Kuber sounds very rationale about his argument.

'Sid has found places in the North part of north Goa, further north of Baga. You are going to the other end. I will sleep it off in our resort at Porvorim, till you both decide on which part of the island you will like to buy. Call me to cut the ribbon at your hotel entrance, and all I will charge, will be an all you can eat buffet at the Park Hyatt. Not at your Dollar Sai's hotel!' Dinshaw smiles trying to look wicked but plays the devil's advocate perfectly; looking like a cute soft toy instead.

Kuber scolds, '*Properdee, properdee, properdee* Dinshaw, land makes more money than apartments, I have explained that to your friend Sid, but the Londoner in him wants to sleep on a bed, high up in the air.'

'Just a small holiday home is all I want, away from the hustle and bustle, the noise of Mumbai. We are choking there with bad air,' responds Sid.

'Boss, I am rooted to the ground, and just here for fun and frolic with you guys. What you both want to do all the time with money, money, money? Chill and relax.' Dinshaw sits back, and bites into the *chickoo*, popping the seeds back into his hand from his mouth, and juggling them like marbles in his hands.

Kuber looks at him with disapproval, that further eggs on Dinshaw, to pop another full *chickoo* in his mouth. 'This man has an appetite of a gorilla,' he mutters to Sid.

Sid's eyes pop out. It is barely the start of the trip and both these friends are dear to him.

Dinshaw takes no objection and simply laughs it off, after popping the seed into his hand and continuing his leg pulling of Kuber, 'We were all apes once upon a time, at least then there were no dollars and money to be made, Mr. Dollar Sai..Dollar, dollar, dollar.' Dinshaw apes a panting dog, without calling Kuber that.

Sid changes the topic, 'Look at the colours of Goa, the blue skies, the red soil and brick structure of houses, the blood orange sun-sets, the tropical fruits, the cashew and feni, the churches, everything so different from Mumbai. The pristine air, clean to breathe and inhale.'

'A lady called Shalomi at a wine shop on my last trip told me, that if you inhale the cashew spirit of feni over a small fire, and breathe in breathe out, it is the best thing for your lungs. That's what all the Goans do, living in the humid climate' says a concerned Dinshaw.

Kuber ribs Dinshaw, 'Dinshaw must be looking at his small hands, and Shalomi's big jugs I am sure...ha ha ha! Trust him to fall for a story from a lady selling wine. Looking else where huh...huh?huh?'

'Leave him alone. For God's sake, she must be your aunt's age Kuber,' cuts in Sid.

Dinshaw turns a bright pink in the face as if he is really caught looking, and nearly wants to ask, 'How did you know?'

He also wonders if Kuber's aunt has big jugs. He keeps quiet, as he hides his thoughts, and turns pink due to that. He finally stops eating his *chickoos,* placing the uneaten ones into a plastic bag.

Kuber explains, like he is their tutor in school, 'They just over grow the cashew and when they don't sell it, they drink and inhale it. There is nothing exotic about it. You should have got off the Chiplun station and you will see all the poor people selling Chickoo milkshakes for less than fifty rupees. It is the same story with mangoes and oranges in Ratnagiri. The Local Alphanso fruit, is a king only in Mumbai, not at the farms where it grows and rots in a good harvest. You both are such suckers and believers in anything. Someone could sell the smaller island of South Goa to you and you would buy it.'

'Which one?' asks Sid, feigning seriousness. He takes this new chemistry, this kind of bonhomie very seriously. He is on the trip more for that, than any land investment.

Pat comes the reply from Kuber, 'The monkey island.'

'That is apt for you to buy, and swing from one tree to another, for the rest of your life.' Dinshaw says this with a dead pan expression, and looks away outside the window, as if to request Sid to change topics as fast as the changing scenery outside.

The train slows down before it reaches it's final destination.

All three of them feel grubby, and the load of the journey starts to weigh on them.
Dinshaw lets out a small fart, and acts as if it was not him.

Kuber continues to dig his nose when he thinks no one is watching, while Sid continues to stroke his new appendage, the thick moustache.

The friends eventually hail a large rickshaw when the train reaches Madgaon station, Sid acknowledges, 'It is indeed a very different experience by train. The ride is not bumpy by road, but it will take some time.'

The rickshaw driver chips in, '*Susegaad Goa sirr, no one in hurry sirrr,* you will be there in an hour.'

'Just don't fall asleep while driving.' replies Dinshaw. He takes his two fingers to pinch his nose.

'Feni Dinshaw, the cashew feni!' smiles Kuber.

Sid laughs it off, admiring the wet green fields.

It has rained in Goa, and everywhere you see, it is a green carpet, the edge of the roads have moss, the edge of the fields have tall green grass and weeds growing, the fields have stalks of barley flailing in the wind. The trees hustle in the breeze that pushes back the hair for all three in the rickshaw, beyond their different sized foreheads.

Sid straightens his dark black moustache with his right hand, and clicks photographs with his cell phone. 'DinDin, you have something to say?'

Dinshaw breaks into a song, tapping his thumb and forefingers on his small stroller sized suitcase.

> *"I was gone in Goa,*
> *no goal, meri hai*
> *... just gone.*

Gone to goa, gone to Goa, Goa meri hai!

Gone to drink,
and speak to the wind.
I hear the air,
hitting my chin.
Gone to goa, gone to Goa, Goa meri hai!

I can smell the grass,
I will smoke the cashew.
Maybe grow a beard
Why be a Mumbai statue?
Gone to goa, gone to Goa, Goa meri hai!"

Kuber smiles and relaxes a bit.

He quietly glances over both the friends, 'I admire your spontaneity, and camaraderie. Let us hope I remain your friend, through thick and thin.'

He too now gazes out at the wet fields, filled with water till the top, a buffalo entirely immersed with its head just appearing afloat. 'I want to be able to sit inside the water of life, without swimming, static, afloat, happy. Like that.' He points at the buffalo.

'You are too lush, luscious my friend, too hungry, to sit like a buffalo. More like a monkey jumping from tree to tree. Hey, hey, ho, ho, ha, ha!' goes Dinshaw.

He begins to drum a tune again, on the handle-bar of the rickshaw driver's back, who also starts to sway to the tune like the palm trees along the winding roads.

"Oye, I am gone in Goa
wanna be drunken silly, silly, silly

Gone to goa, gone to Goa, Goa meri hai!

Oye I'm gone to Goa,
Look at the women, (he waves to the passerby women, who
surprisingly wave back and smile)
sweet like a lily, lily, lily.
Gone to goa, gone to Goa, Goa meri hai!

Oye I'm gone to Goa,
Why should I go back?
Let us just sleep on the beach,
and have wines, rack after rack.
Gone to goa, gone to Goa, Goa meri hai!

Oye I am gone in Goa
wanna be drunken silly, silly, silly.
Gone to goa, gone to Goa, Goa meri hai!"

He pulls at Kuber, and gives him a hug, and attempts to give him a brotherly kiss. It turns Kuber red in the face, into a shy corner of the rickshaw. He pushes Dinshaw away.

Dinshaw looks at him, 'What happened my Dollar Sai? I am just having some fun, why do you run? Ha ha ha...'

The rickshaw turns into the corner of their resort.

'Stop stop stop,' shouts Kuber, and jumps out. Before paying, he walks away into the gate of the resort.

The other two friends scratch their heads, surprised to see him in a hurry, perhaps trying to avoid paying.

'I will pay Sid, you go pick up the beers. Don't you find him a bit odd?' Dinshaw asks Sid.

'And the feni DinDin,' replies Sid in the affirmative and nods at Dinshaw.

As Sid walks toward the wine shop, a coconut falls from above, a couple of feet away from him. 'That could have been my skull, cracked wide open.'

'Hey lucky you!' shouts out Dinshaw, 'Nothing will upset our plans to have fun this trip.'

Sid just waves back. He rides his luck lightly.

Ψ

The next morning they wake up, coming out of their rooms in shorts and tee-shirts. Dinshaw has a beer bottle in his hand, walking toward the swimming pool.

Sid carries the feni bottle in his hand, 'You wish to try?' he asks Kuber.

Kuber does not reply, looking glum and lost within himself.

'What's up? Everything looking good back home?'

'Yes.' replies Kuber. 'Could have been better with Rekha.' he mentions this to Sid, ensuring that Dinshaw is out of range to listen. 'The marriage is broken, but I thought Rekha will remain a friend. It does not look like that now.'

'Relax you guys, loosen up a little, have a shot with lime.' says Dinshaw.

'You know me DinDin, I have given up drinks since three years now,' Sid quite sure of himself, 'I got this for Kuber, as I thought he may want to give it a try.'

'So Sid, what do you think about the hotel plot I was talking about. It is close to Colva, and we can hire a cab from the resort and be there in half an hour, while your pal here Dinshaw can pour himself some beers and sleep it off in Porvorim.'

Dinshaw says, 'I will join too in the excursion, but will not be able to invest. Land is not my cup of tea.'

Kuber grimaces, feeling that Dinshaw is impacting Sid's thinking.

'I will not buy into anything, if as my friends you both will not take a joint decision with me,' Sid inhales a deep gulp of of air, 'No point coming here and living alone in an apartment, the resort is enough for that.'

Kuber seems more disappointed, 'See it once, that is all I ask. Then maybe I make an offer, that is too good to refuse.'

PART – 3.

The Bogey

20. Anti-Climax

A figure of speech, used to satire or ridicule. It is a sudden descent from higher to lower importance.

Illustration:

Who cares what was the religion of the occupiers in Goa! Today it is just a tourist hot spot.

20. The trap

While Dinshaw is enjoying his siesta in the afternoon, Sid and Kuber end up taking the resort taxi toward Colva.

As they drive past the sights and enter south Goa, Sid is lost in his own thoughts.

Kuber descends from the cab, and signals to the agent waiting outside the San Thome Museum. He talks with the agent in whispers, and re-boards the cab to continue the journey toward Sebastien Chapel.

Eventually the cab stops near a large reddish-brown soil spot, 'This soil reminds me of our school picnic holiday in Matheran,' blurts out Sid. 'Your antics not withstanding.'

Kuber smirks at that comment, 'Thank God you won't be turning the monkeys on me here.'

Sid 'Hey, you never know. Something about this place, the foot-ball ground opposite this land, the sea-shore is giving me a deep sense of deja-vu. It makes me feel I was always here.'

Kuber smiles a weak, 'Finally!' and walks ahead with the agent, onto the land.

'See from here you can observe the tourists take the aerial route into the sea, tied to the sea-boats. This land has a natural elevation, so the sea breeze will hit us till the second floor of our resort, once we build it. I intend to use all the soil and give it a red-brick structure. The red-clay is used to make the bricks, giving it a very distinct Goan look to the properties that use it.'

Kuber's agent assures Sid, 'The traditional red bricks. They use to make houses in Goa.' Sid looks him up and down.

The agent introduces himself, 'I Stanley sir. Kuber Sir agent sir. It can be meshed and used as a mix with stone also sir.'

Sid ignores Stanley, 'Why this piece of land?' he addresses the question to Kuber.

Stanley chips in again, 'I live behind museum, you can come again any time to view land. The local fisherman lady called Tia, who used to own it. She die after her son was find dead on sea-shore at beach. It be same day the Portuguese were make to leave by Government of the India. So her land remain un-claimed for long. Indian government take very long sire.'

Sid looks Stanley up and down more seriously now. 'Go on.'

'Very long to know she and her son were originally Indians. Not really East Indians. Though they go by the names of Noronha, they were trace to originally be Brahmins Sir. Though they do some small agriculture on this land, they were mostly use it for fishing. Also her son be so fond of tortoise, he would make sure eggs they laid under rocky cliffs, always had a chanced to survive.' Stanley ends his mixed up grammar - very happy with himself, to have shared the folklore with someone, who did not know it.

After all, Sid was not from the village.

'Slow and steady, does not win the race after all.' smiled Kuber.

'He is right, the original Konkan Brahmin names are registered in the property as *Hattangadis*. It goes back to a small piece of paper on the bark of a coconut tree, and some other papers signed up in some Portuguese dialect. Their forefathers converted, after the French left from Bombay's seven islands, and the Portuguese occupied and took over the spice trade of India.

'Why are they called East Indians, if they were still from here, the western part of India?' asks a puzzled Sid.

The taxi driver who is in ear-shot, walks up, 'May I sir? My name Vaz sir.' Sid nods an affirmation.

Vaz speaks softly in a cultured manner, 'They were actually converted by the descendants of the Ancient Christian community, over five hundred years ago; by descendants of Bartholomew, who was one of the descendants of the twelve apostles of Jesus, according to the new testament. They were better known as Nathaniels earlier, and they were known to have sailed for trade of spices, cheese, - even salt. Some of them were butchers. They coalesced under the Portuguese rule and came to be known as Norteiros and Noronhas eventually. They perhaps came with the Portuguese Christians or Bombay Portuguese to Goa with the British from Bombay.'

Kuber too is now listening intently. He is happy that the story of Vaz Driver has made the land look more authentic than what just the papers show.

Vaz continues acting like a Goan guide, 'The province in the north, based at Fort San Sebastian of Bassein, was evangelized by the Franciscans originally. They belonged to the order of the Catholic Church, founded in 1200's by the Francis of Assisi, who was really only a poet and mystic.'

Sid is now hooked, 'Go on Vaz.'

'It was in 52AD, when Thomas Apostle sailed to what they knew as the Malabar region, else till then it was the Varmas in Kerala sir.'

The driver has joined in and taken over the conversation, without others realizing when he had walked toward Stanley.

He seems to be the most educated of the lot, on the history of Goans. 'It all started from Kerala sir, from where the religion was spread by way of conversions, how do we know who we are, we are merely human, and off course Goan! First and last Goan sir. The rest is just history and accidental conversions.'

'Varmas were in rule in Kerala around 1800's. I think you are mixed up. However, religion changes, when rulers change' says Kuber matter of factly. 'What is it to us? Who cares what was the religion of the occupiers in Goa! Today it is just a tourist hot spot.'

Opportunism reeking from him like a local Goan's breath of alcohol. There is greed in the eye, where the dreams of Kuber take seed. He is a pure mercenary.

'Dollar Sai has spoken,' says Sid winking at Vaz driver, remembering Dinshaw missing from the land site. 'Dinshaw must be having his sweet siesta. Let us head back.'

Stanley continues, 'There be no other claimant of the land sir. The government attached the land and passed it to the Reconstruction Asset company of Goa, and freed the title from other Goans, as the land be earmarked for a hotel property. The next door church provide the local touch, and the sea of tourists that the government wants comes to South Goa for some peace and the quiet. North Goa now be fill up with tourists and Russian sponsored druggies.'

'Besides this beach? Any other sandy spots here?' asks a curious Sid. 'I usually holiday in North Goa.'

'There is Majorda, there is Benaulim. Made famous by Sunset Deck and ZeeBop. There is also Varca further south.'

'Kuber there are already quite a few hotels, Hyatt is there at the top end, there is Royal Orchid and so many other small lodge villas. Why not take up one or two of the ready made local villas?' asks Sid, still circumspect.

He walks and ambles around the edge of the cliff, toward the beach below and the sea-shore.

He looks around in all directions of the beach, the afternoon sun. His long-distance glasses get coloured with the sun, due to their photo-chromatic lens.

His vision still clear, his mind is in a blur.

'Land is land Sid, we will make a killing. Later we can transfer the hotel on a long lease to a top hotel chain, who can run the property for us.'

'Very good plan sir,' chips in Stanley. This time Kuber stares him down, and gesticulates him to walk away back toward the taxi.

Stanley goes and walks toward the taxi-driver on the other side of the cliff.

Kuber and Sid sit on the edge of the cliff, which has a slightly small ledge below it, to break the steep fall. The sea breeze is strong, and a whiff of the coastal salty air smudges the sunglasses of Sid.

He takes them down to wipe the glass, with the inner fold of his shirt bottom.

Kuber looks on serenely towards the sea. 'You remember, in Mumbai we had spoken about our thought of naming our company Serenity Hotels. The land could be used to create an old age home, a place for senior people care too, if not a hotel.'

'Let me sleep on it,' reflects Sid

'Sure, there is no hurry. I have fixed the paper-work. It is already in my hands, once you say yes, I will secure it under the company. Your money will be used to issue you the shares in our company.'

Before getting on the way back to the resort, Sid decides to break the journey for a coffee.

'Let me pick something up for Dinshaw.' The two of them walk across the football field toward La Rosa cafe. The owner is a lady wearing a brown dress, her dark hands a shade darker than her sandals; she places two cups of Nescafe brewed in a milk concoction before the two of them.

Sid gazes at her hands, her forehead, it looks very similar to a lady he thinks he has seen before, but he cannot place her.

Again a sense of deja vu overwhelms him. He remains silent.

In the background is a lilting tune coming from Beno Cafe, a place they did not walk to, 'Bum bum bum bum, come to Goa, come to Goa, Goa merry hai, Goa Amchi re!' The tune, is very very catchy and yet very nostalgic. It is sung in a melodious way like Dinshaw the previous day, and is lilting its way to his coffee cup.

Sid feels he has heard the tune before, infinite number of times.

It sets him thinking of some past images, pictures in his mind, that he cannot place, a fishing village, boats, the sandy beaches, flappy turtles and eggs.

Sid gazes at the framed photograph of shells on the wall, and the tortoise shape tin, in which Ms. Rosa appears to be placing bills of rupees and some coins.

A toothless customer, with greying hair is sitting and eating a mango coloured pulp, that resembles the shape of a caramel custard pudding. He suddenly calls out, 'Rosa, one more.'

Behind Ms. Rosa are packs of jelly, custard with names like Blue bird and Rex written on them. A timeless black and white picture of Mario graces the wall, with a similar toothless man eating a *Serradura*, with layers of whipped cream over it.

The man below the picture looks like he has been sitting exactly there for a hundred years, and eating the same dish, wearing as he is the same clothes. A white shirt and a black pant, as depicted in the picture above him. The bright mango coloured fruit is the only dash of colour in the otherwise black and white spot.

Sid unconsciously stares at Ms. Rosa and the tortoise shaped coin collecting tin while sipping his coffee.

Kuber opposite him asks if he is done, when Sid orders another coffee to take-away. As they step out of the cafe, they see a man, sitting in a yellow coloured vest.

Kuber shouts out, 'G'dbye Uncle.'

'I not your uncle.' spits out the old man. He has a tilted rusted tin board saying, *F.X. Periera's Restaurant*, with different prices of Fish Masala Fry, Prawns Vindaloo, Mackerel Rechado, Fish curry and Chicken Cafreal listed with unheard of prices.

'You serve food sir? Can I take away?' asks Kuber in not his usual style, being ultra polite.

'Shut down, get lost.' replies the man.

Driver Vaz tells Kuber, 'Never mind sir, the ol'drunk has nothing to do. He is just grumpy, he just sit there whole day. Do nothing. Look at cars and bikers come and go.'

'The prices must have looked very attractive to Kuber,' says Sid to Stanley, his agent.

Kuber laughs it off, and speaks to Stanley, 'I am so miserly, I can kill the mosquito that bites my blood, to get his blood also back. Interest on my principal.'

'That should keep your money safe sir,' nudges an over zealous Stanley to Sid.

Kuber cautions Stanley to stay quiet, and asks Vaz to drive back to the resort.

'Let's go!' is all Kuber ends with.

21. Deja Vu

Dinshaw has hit the bed early, having hit the bottles of beer and then feni quite early since evening. Sid and Kuber find him sloshed when they return, and order an early dinner.

Tired with the sunny and humid weather, they retire to their individual rooms.

That night, at the Cashavella Resort, Sid gets a deja vu dream.

He can see a lady figure, behind the living and dining room area where he is seated. He can see her cook something and then, walk to the table with a few dishes. There is Fish Fry, Chicken Cafreal and Mackereal Rechado, with little tags on toothpicks pointing out of the meat, labelling the dishes.

Sid speaks aloud in his dream, 'I cannot eat all this.'

From across the table, comes a voice, 'Shut up, eat, or get lost.' It is the same man from the cafe, from Mario's painting, wearing the white shirt and black pant.

Instead of the mango, he has a massive half piece of mackerel in his plate, the other half on a spoon. An orange curry splattered all over the table-cloth before him.

Sid sniffs, 'It smells like *Goan Bangda* curry,' he can get a distinct smell of coconut gravy, with his sharpened sense of smell. Yet he also realizes he is asleep, he wonders how his senses are active, he smacks his lips getting the distinct flavour.

'Shhh....' says the mother. '*My porga*, my son, let me tell you a secret, I am Tia. Your mother from past life. You remember the chapel at Velha Goa? We always used to pray on Sundays, we meet with all the village people there every Sunday.'

'Mother Mary?' quizzes Sid.

'No, no, your mother. Mother Tia. You remember you were hurt in football? Hidden behind the trees on the land they show you today, is the same spot, where the concrete chairs used to exist. They still do. You were hurt there.'

'I can still feel the pain in my abdomen, now that you talk about it. Go on...' says Sid, his milky white eyes now partly open in his dark room.

The crimson orange coloured gravy gets hazy on the table cloth. It seems to appear like dried blood. 'I can see waves of a beach, I have fallen from some height, it feels like a sinking feeling. I see a tortoise staring back at me. Or is it a turtle?'

Tia continues talking to him, 'Dug in the pit there, ten feet below the concrete chairs, is a Portuguese trunk filled with gold coins from the era when we were Hattangadi, not Noronha. Over three centuries old.'

'Tree trunk? Gold coins???' Sid feels the shock in his sleep.

'No no. Portmanteau, a steamer trunk. There is a turtle shell and leather on it. Some of these coins are from the British and Portuguese time, brought on ships from there. You need to be careful of your closest friend here, it was the same thing last time I warn you, you never listen to me.'

'I never listen to you? I do not know you.' replies Sid, talking as if in a hypnotic trance. 'You talking about Dinshaw, aapla DinDin? Or Kuber?'

'Go there, look for it yourself, go alone. Otherwise, with the treasure your life will be lost. I warn you, I warn you. Listen to mother Tia. You not listen to me my son. Last time, you no listen.'

Ψ

Sid wakes up from his deep sleep to find himself seated before his room window, over-looking some palm trees. The violet peach hues of the sky, suggest to him an early dawn.

'I usually don't get dreams, this one is about some coins, in a turtle trunk.' He scratches his head.

He wonders, from where this all originates, the lilting music last evening, the old Uncle eating mango, his vivid dream of the same uncle eating Mackerel. Mother Tia?? Past life? What is this, deja vu?

'Really!? Have I reincarnated? Mother Tia? Really?' Sid shakes his head to himself.

Sid fails to co-relate the tortoise tin, the trunk, the Rosa Cafe owner and the dream he has got. He speaks about it to Dinshaw in the morning over break-fast, who laughs it off.

Dinshaw sneers, 'This is what happens when you don't cool off on a few beers.'

Dinshaw speaks up, when Kuber joins them, 'This man now has Mother Mary and some old drunkard eating fish coming in his dreams.'

Kuber just looks on silently at Sid, hoping he would commence the talk about the land, but holds it back. He has Stanley on his mobile phone, whom he blows away, 'Will call you later in the evening.'

Sid describes whatever he remembers of the dream. 'I tell you before, I feel I have come here at some earlier time, I cannot place this deja vu correctly.'

Dinshaw's phone rings, and it appears to be an emergency call from home.

Kuber tells him, 'You were here last time with Prahlad and Yug, perhaps these are memories from that trip.' Sid remains anguished and falls silent, munching on his oats straining them from his cereal filled milk.

Kuber devours his masala omelette. He too falls silent.

Dinshaw finishes his call, 'I will have to head back to Mumbai today. There has been a near calamity in my family, my father has taken very ill and I have to head back today itself. My brother has just hospitalized him at Nanavati hospital.'

Dinshaw just abruptly leaves his break-fast table and moves toward the door to head back to the room.

'We understand.' says Kuber.

'Dinshaw, do you want us...?' Sid asks...before he completes Dinshaw replies, 'You complete the trip, I will meet you guys back in Mumbai.'

Kuber is ecstatic, but hides his excitement.

He waits till Sid looks back at him. He smiles, 'Referring to your dream, the only way to find out is to head back to the land.'

Sid nods.

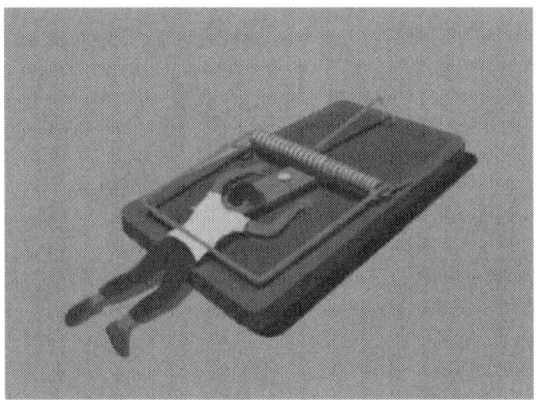

22. The unfathomable loss.

Dinshaw places the receiver from his home telephone instrument down. He is aghast, his face turns ashen. His brother at the other end of the sofa asks him, 'What happened, Dinshaw?'

'It is not possible, I cannot believe it,' rues Dinshaw

'What??' asks his brother.

'We have lost Sid,' Dinshaw's words fall out of his mouth, more out of remorse rather than any audible expression.

'What!!!' exclaims his brother.

'Sid fell off a cliff it seems, yesterday when he was viewing a parcel of land, with Kuber. I just cannot believe it.' Dinshaw is shaking his head left to right, and right to left.

'A cliff?? This sounds so unbelievable like in the movies,' says his brother. The loss is more for Dinshaw to face, as his brother is more concerned for their own father's poor health currently.

'Kuber just called me, he had obtained signatures the previous day, after I left Goa. Sid was, Sid was supposed to...' he trails off. 'My God, I cannot believe it. I have to now call and inform Simi.'

The devastation that the news of Sid's demise causes, spreads like a depression ripple the next day. All the goodness done, comes back to Simi' doorstep.

Her children rally around her and fly down from London. Yug takes over all the ceremonial rituals. He pays for the necessary expenses and manages the priest, arranges the flowers, ties the thatched makeshift stretcher, with bamboo sticks.

Som Sarkaar is broken. He cannot stop sobbing, he carries the *dhoop and incense* sticks, their smoke, clouding his eyes further.

Kuber is heard gossiping over the phone to Prahlad, 'Yug has spent all the cash, I don't know if he will get the money back from Simi. It will go down the drain,' he waits for an answer.

Prahlad offers none.
He has heard from Yug before, that Kuber is spreading false rumours about him and his father.

He is well aware of this duplicate nature of Kuber, so he offers no response. While listening to him he in fact sends a clarification message on whatAp to both Som Sarkaar and Yug Ikani, creating a mourning group of all friends of Sid. It includes Dinshaw, and Prahlad leaves Kuber out of that group.

Sarkaar replies to Prahald, 'There are rumours here, of something fishy having taken place in Goa. Yet Kuber has spread his version of different rumours. He has employed the driver from Goa, and made Vaz spread conversations to all other drivers.'

'Messy,' replies Prahlad, 'I'm staying out of it.'

Sarkaar writes, 'Rekha had warned me, that Kuber will have his vengeance some time, but I still never expected betrayal and deceit toward Sid. He was the only one who was backing Kuber's dreams, spending time with him, giving him a shoulder to cry on.'

'It is what it is.' It is the reply from Prahlad.

Sarkaar notes the indifference, and spends time explaining the whole opposite version of rumours to Yug.

Yug detaches himself to feel the sorrow less, 'I can't take all this Sarkaar, I am in no shape, at least not now. Let me get all this through first. I have so much tension at work, and Diya also has issues at home currently with me.'

Sarkaar probes, 'Will you do nothing about it? Simi is not saying anything, but Sid's money is riding on Kuber's venture, and he is saying nothing about his share, or what they may have found on the land. Sid had spoken about it to Dinshaw...'

Yug replies nonchalantly, 'Dinshaw will talk everything only in line with what Sid would have told him, no doubt about that. But money is the first thing that comes in between friends.'

'Money was the only thing Kuber every cared about,' complains Sarkaar. 'Sid was the only one who understood the loss of my wife, the loss of my mother. He would listen to his friends. He was the only one who took the path of fairness, took decisions and still kept us united, despite controversies.'

Yug determines that the priest will take more time, 'Call the ambulance toward the gate of the apartment block,' he shouts out to the security guard. He continues talking to Sarkaar, 'So

Sid should have avoided or not got entangled with Kuber then. He knew how he was since school days. There was enough to know about his business dealings and antics too, his affairs, his behaviour with his own folks, with Rekha. What more was needed to warn and keep Sid away?'

'I had thought Dinshaw had accompanied them to Goa, so he would have taken care of mutual interests. He had to fly back...all is lost now, we have lost our friend, I have lost my dearest pal.' Sarkaar starts sobbing.

The nature of the loss now dawns on Yug's emotions too, and he cracks up as well. There are silent tears flowing out of his eyes. Yug remembers the college days academic time spent together. The key time they spent in evaluating his decision to marry. Then after that their paths meandered. Yug holds himself, wiping away his grief quickly.

Sid's son, carrying the Hindu pot of incense sticks, representing the spirit soul, leads the stretcher to which a beaming Sid is tied under layers of white sheets and silky shawls.

Sid is clean shaven as always, and *tilaks* of saffron, and turmeric on his forehead make him look like the serene sun, setting at the horizon of calm white waters.

Simi insists that Kuber be told to leave. She and Dinshaw trail the ambulance in their car.

Kuber with sullen guilty eyes, follows their car nevertheless, hidden a few cars behind the trail of vehicles leading to the cremation grounds.

Sid's daughter is inconsolable, as she is left sitting with her grand-mother at the apartment block.

While the life of a friend has come to an end, not many know, while carrying his body, that his soul has been left behind in Goa.

His spirit, bonding with Tia and the past story of his original mother land, has found solace in Goa.

Of little consequence to him is the treasure trunk and the fact that his friend has caused this deceit in a second life time.

Sadly, Kuber Savla has not found liberation in re-birth. Nor has he honoured the past bonhomie.

Yet, the betrayal is not lost on Sid's soul.

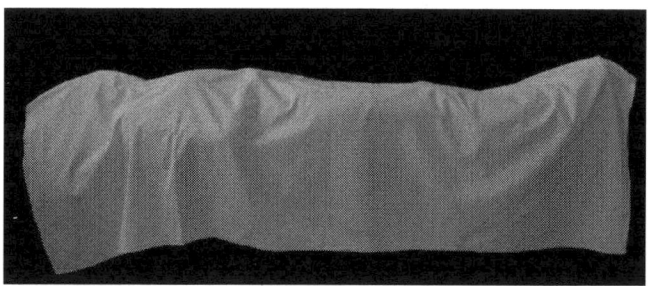

23. A broken man

A few months after Sid's demise in Goa, Dinshaw loses his father.

A fan of leading his life without any encumbrance, care or control, his father succumbs with acute diabetes to a heart attack, a common critical illness among Indians.

Dinshaw, a broken man, cannot step out of his house for days, which convert into weeks, and months. Everyone around him is worried for him.

He stops eating sugary foods, and gradually other foods as well. He reduces his diet and sheds over twenty kilos of weight.

Nothing has changed for Dinshaw, except inheriting a huge estate from his father and the upkeep of his brother and his own family. Looking visibly distraught on most days, he attempts to look facially different, growing a moustache.

He introspects a lot, as his father's loss, gives him a sense of deprivation – the lack of a family. He increasingly begins the process of growing inwards. Dinshaw begins to feel that no one around him understands him any more.

It is too much for Dinshaw to take the loss of his father after the loss of his friend. 'Would he have preferred it the other way around? Someone should have survived for him to mourn his loss, so that he could have cried his heart out. He has lost both, his father and his friend, delivering a solid blow.

He becomes reserved and finds a sense of emptiness hitting his vacant life.

He begins to visit temples, spiritual places and tours extensively via train to his place of birth in North India, to find himself, a new sense of identity. He conducts many home based rituals, prayer ceremonies and even attends sermons presided by a visiting monk at home and the suburban temple.

After a few months, some friends meet him and say, 'Eat, drink and make merry DinDin.' The name was used extensively by Sid, but now everyone uses it.

This makes Dinshaw more glum than ever. '*Go to Goa, Go to goa, Goa meri hai...*' rings in his ears.

His soul hums the tune that is stuck in his head.

A close scouts friend finally helps to put balm on his emotional wounds, 'Rest assured Dinshaw, your father went without any suffering. It ended in a few minutes for him. Imagine if he was in hospital and you would have to take care of him over a prolonged illness.'

Time flies.

Dinshaw's moustache grows thicker, other than that, all his life pursuits and interests grow thinner.

Eventually a year elapses, Dinshaw begins to commence his own spiritual journey, leading to an immaterial existence.

He believes that while he is alive, charitable causes for the differently abled and promoting sport for the under privileged, will give him peace and happiness.

Yet at the back of his mind, he is in a state of shock over his friends' demise. He had never really recovered having lost someone from his own age group, when his father also passed away.

The loss of both has compounded his grief. His soul is in a permanent state of turmoil.

Melancholy sinks in.

He considers the double whammy situation to be unfortunate; yet he cannot fathom the reason why someone like Sid, would end his own life, jumping over a cliff.

'It just does not add up,' he repeats to himself, and whoever he meets. '*Go to Goa, goa to Goa, Goa meri hai...*'

The tune is now stuck in his heart.

Due to his sad mental state, no one takes Dinshaw seriously.

He is left alone, to handle the indifference of the rest of the friends, and observes that only Simi like him is impacted deeply.

Dinshaw asks himself every day, 'There are no other friends, there is no friendship. People just don't care, and you have to believe it, accept it, but how do you stop missing your loved ones?'

'Just care a little less DinDin, just care a little less.'

Dinshaw can hear Sid's voice ring in his ears.

'Take care of yourself first, else how will you handle your family?'

24. Kuber's predicament.

Kuber Savla has never been more lonely than on his own birthday that year. He is unable to make any time for his partner, who has lost complete interest in him.

Rekha has come to know about his under-hand methods to grow his business, and the kind of company he keeps.

'I cannot go on waiting, there is so much still to do, rather than take life easy and rest on our laurels.'

After the walk out on Rekha, he had moved in with one of his girl-friends, eventually hiring her for the sales and marketing needs of the project.

'I hate Rekha, and I hate her, and her and her. All of them are the same. They live for themselves, donning their mask of charades and artificiality. They don't know Mr. Fraud himself. Come and fuck with Mr. Fraud. Come, come! Come one, come all.'

Kuber is aware, that his cover over his multiple extra-marital affairs is completely over. He has barely fucked a woman.

He has two girls waiting for the culmination of his marriage promises, a third, a one-time model, waiting for him to open new salons all over Mumbai.

He has currently moved in with a girl with a hotelier background, to suit his immediate business needs, and plans to marry her eventually.

'Maybe not really.' he tells himself. 'Rati, Sapna and Joanna. All the same.'

Joanna due to her hotelier background seems the best bet, but he overlooks her material nature, as he tries to forget Rekha, Yug and Prahald. Sid is long gone. Sarkaar was never his friend.

'They consume me since college. Material, is immaterial my foot! Material can buy a person Prahlad! Material can buy a woman. Material can buy anyone anything.'

To win her over, beyond just wooing her, he purchases a luxury Yacht and parks it in Goa's Mandovi, paying for it's anchorage charges. It makes himself feel more important.

He makes a final submission of plans to build his hotel in Goa, thoughts for which consume him entirely.

'I cannot for the world understand, why the remainder of our friends have deserted me? With Sid, at least he believed in me that much that he would come to Goa, inspect the land and spend some time. Like in London, create some bonhomie time together.'

Kuber has started spending visible public time, talking to himself. Earlier he would do it when there was no one around him. Now the self doubt, the self dialogue starts early evenings over drinks and continues till late at night.

It recurs in Mumbai and on his back and forth trips to Goa.

He takes aimless cycle trips, all over South Goa, riding toward the beaches, and cycles through the fishermen colonies.

He loses his way through ample roads intertwining with sandy spots, the surfy sea, and re-discovers shacks that are given out on license to locals selling their own wines and local brew.

There is Peno's, the Southern Neck, the Ballantine Shack, Cosmos, Khopddi & Khuris, and even a Vegan place for Jains. All of the places dot the beach-front. Kuber has no clue, if he has ever been through these lanes before, he cycles to keep himself fit, and his mind in order. Yet he forgets the routes each time.

He can feel he is occasionally losing it. Often, he loses his cycle and is forced to walk.

He feels the pinch of loneliness and is discomforted by the rejection of his friends.

Post the drinks, he carries a bottle of water mixed with a strong shot of four lemons, and walks it off till he reaches his hotel. He eats four boiled egg whites during his drinks and knocks off to sleep eating two english cucumbers on bread-butter in his room.

He begins to drink heavily starting at the cusp of sunset, over a light brunch and a few light beers at noon. He moves over to vodka shots mixed with beer and rum, continuing till the sun goes down with him.

Kuber does not seem to correctly notice himself. He has few hours of a normal morning, which he wastes shaving and talking to his delusional self in the mirror.

He does not take calls from his mother in Mumbai, disconnecting them repeatedly, and is not keen to meet his family other than on two days of Diwali. That too if he remembers which dates Diwali falls on.

He stops making the to and fro trips to Mumbai, and ends up spending more weeks of every month in Goa. Yet it does not feel like paradise to him. It feels heavy, like his conscience.

Kuber Savla has fallen for the glitz trap of wealth, women and vodka. In the hot weather, without realizing he has had one too many, he sweats at drink tables, and repeats to different waiters, 'I want two more' ordering at the close of dinner time.

That is before his meandering walk along the beach-side, 'I knows the ways likes the backs of my palms.' he hollers once he is drunk at the waiters.

On his walk, he keeps his shirt-buttons open, and talks to himself in mumbo-jumbo. 'I know, I know! I know Prahlaaaaaad, I know you, I know Yuggy, I know you.'

'Prahlad! Stand-up to your father I say.'

'Yug, I know I know you bloody f'cker! No spine, no balls, to try anything different. So many times I talked to your wife also, but you bugger would still not call or talk. More worried for Simi and Sid's kids. Sid ka dost, bloody burnt toast.'

Passerby Israeli tourists, look Kuber up and down, while several British and American tourists walk past him. Two Russians are afar, near some marooned boats. Some women, smoking as they walk, step out from the shacks, to join them for a smoke. Kuber is walking head-on toward them.

'Savla, I say, you can suck the blood of a mosquito, what are these friends worth? Bloodless spineless fuckers. No sharing of vision. Blame game, hate game. A competition from young days, is there anyone for you really in life Kuber Savla? The girls also, want your balls and money ultimately. *Ya ya, ma ya ya, my foot.*'

He walks, keeping up the direction of the waves that break at the wet side of the beach, in and out of the sea. 'Low tide, no friend, high tide, no friend. Is the wave water? Is the foam water? Is this sand? Only salty deposits! Only salty buggers. The material is Material fuckers! It is not immaterial, it is not immaterial.'

He reaches the Russians. The women behind them in sarongs, cigars in hand, look at him with curiosity.

With red eyes, Kuber spews his feelings to strangers, 'Truth is, this is my place, Goa. I belong here. I was here before anyone else. Anyone!'

He points at the white caucasian males to walk away toward the land. 'You Portuguesa f'ckers go away. To your flaming Vasco Casco past.'

'I'm Putin.' says one.
'I'm Gorbachov' says the other.

The Russians stand tall, as they know they control and supply the beach they stand on, via their drug mafia, and take him for the drunk he is.

'Then I'm Trump you f'ckers.'

The Russians break into loud laughter.

Kuber kneels before them, and speaks aloud in drunken stupor.

> *'Where boats don't bait, they stay docked.*
> *Skies don't lie,*
> *and Men don't fly,*
> *They float!*
>
> *Even crows don't sing,*
> *they talk.*
> *Guvaaa, where Truth is simply*
> *buried in the sand.'*

'Should I pound him into the sand?' says Gorbachov. The ladies decline. So does Putin.

The women continue to gaze at him, with a sense of pity. It is getting pitch dark now. The only light is from the tips of the Russian cigars and their cigarettes. Their men look at Kuber with disdain, and don't take him to be a wee bit of a threat.

There is smoke and a fermented aroma of cigar smell in the air. It clouds Kuber's brains further.

Unsteady, Kuber Savla gets up and first walks toward them, instead of walking on the land abutting the beach. 'Fuck them, let them all die like rats. Not everyone has the heart like me. They are just apes. That is the model of their dead lives.'

'Find a friend pal, find a friend, you gonna fall.' The Russian warns him, and walks away. He gesticulates toward the duty officer at the life-guard post.

'And who the fuck are you? Could not find a friend, a single friend, since school, a bit too late now.' Kuber remembers Sid glumly. 'If only the fool was still there, at least there would be someone for me to fox.'

One of the Russians walk up to Kuber, and look him in the eye.

That puts the sense of fear in his brains, that a small brown monkey has if a tall white gorilla is looking down at him. Kuber knows he can be pounded into the sand, which will take a crane to lift him out of the beach.

One of the two males, just nudges at his shoulder, and Kuber falls in a heap on the wet part of the low tide sand. New waves come and hit and collide on his back, his shorts wet.

He pees in his wet pants, all the vodka and beer held in his bladder peters out.

It empties out in the white foam of the sea, forming its own cocktail.

It was the year 2025, and Kuber had no friend, no visitor, no one he knew from his school friends or anyone else, who came to visit him in Goa.

'What was it all for? Just myself. I used to love them, now I hate them, I hate him.'

Fear mixes with hatred inside him, and he holds onto it.

25. Metonymy

A figure of speech, in which one word, is used to refer to something related to that thing.

Illustration:
He was our true Buddha, our Siddhartha.

The father is buddha below the tree.

25. Penultimate
(25 years later, 2050)

The fruit always falls near the tree.

A child, close to his mother, falls at her feet eventually. The *mother*, is the bark of the banyan tree in India, she provides nourishment and an upbringing to the child. The *father*, is Buddha, below that tree.

Mothers and fathers usually do a fabulous job with their children, especially in India where family is the core of existence.

The rest is the *environment or the school* the children go to, and the *company* they kept.

Kuber Savla had missed out in all the areas. It was their company he hoped that would salvage him.

Sarkaar had a Buddha in his father.

Prahlad Ahuja had grown older, in his American *environment,* while Yug behaved at times as if he was still young at heart and in *school*.

'A train journey via Ratnagiri is the most scenic ride on the Konkan railways, even after sixty years.' gushes Kuber.

'Taking this journey is the only thing that can give peace to his soul. And mine. It is not for the money. We could have flown down,' says Yug.

Prahlad adds, 'I always used to say, the material, is immaterial. I had it all, as a kid too, still I had nothing.' Prahlad has carried his emptiness around since childhood.

'Oh Prahlad, stop it man.' quips Sarkaar. 'Only you with your providence can say that. The rest of us had to earn our living.'

'You will never understand.' Prahlad returns to his despondent self.

Yug interjects, 'Take it easy Sarkaar, even Sid's buddy Dinshaw used to say that. We used to listen to music together; they both used to love Elton John's *Sacrifice*.'

'The bugger died on us man' hisses Prahlad. 'We left it for too late. It has been over two and half decades since he has gone. I still miss him.'

Sid had passed long back, and these friends had waited till they each touched 80 to make a reunion trip again. Prahlad had hoped that everyone's temperament would have held up; his real reason to visit, was to give his daughter a trip to India and show her, his roots. He had left her behind in Mumbai with his sister.

Sarkaar flinches, 'He had told me, he wanted to live till 92. he was full of life. God takes away the best. My wife went early too. Too early. I had hoped we would celebrate the year 2050 together. Now I will be with you morons this new year eve.'

Som Sarkaar was the first one to inch toward 80, rest of the three of them were still 79 technically as their birthdays came later that new year.

Numbers and age, was not the only thing that Som Sarkaar was thoughtful about.

Kuber frowned as always. He let's out a grumpy groan. 'Grow out of it, it's been years now. You all still remember the fool? His ghost will be roaming around us in this train and listening. He would be laughing at all of you. I say we throw a party and celebrate that we are alive. Look, I am opening my fifth hotel in Siolim. It was Sid's favourite destination. We can have a celebration.'

'He had all the time in his life for us, we let him down. He kept telling me, that it was me who had no time. Yet I could never find time from work to relent. He always wanted an encore to the school trip.' Yug wipes his eyes dry, before the tears that have welled up fall out on his wrinkled face.

Prahlad says, 'I did not want to come to India. It plays up on my health, and my travels never end without a long bout of coughing and weeks of sickness. It would have been so much better to meet in Manhattan.' He takes out some wet wipes and places one on his face, and the other two are used to wipe his long arms.

The quiet Som Sarkaar gets upset, 'Can we show some respect? Can we just complete what we had started out to do thirty years back? What's the point of all your success if you cannot keep time to pay homage to Sid? I came from Navsari hoping that you all don't start this diatribe and grumbling again. Sid was the only one who really cared for each of us. He never let us fall or suffer. He thought about each of our kids, including the lack of Kuber's.'

'We hear you now Sarkaar, thank you very much,' complains Kuber. 'He was always interested to play today's Gandhi, so he had to go early. Carrying ideals and principles of a hundred years ago. Now please shut up.'

'He was our true Buddha, our Siddhartha.' says Sarkaar fondly.

'That's a bit much. Look guys, I am done with quarrelling with each one of you. I came, because Prahlad is here from the US of A,' claims Yug.

'You mean from Dallas,' interjects Prahlad, monopolizing Yug as always.

'Just bugger off back to your US of A, you have not got me a cent of funding for my hotels, go get some funding for your old friend' cribs Kuber. 'And spend more time with your wife, she keeps complaining about you.'

Muttering below his breath, 'The selfish, the most material man, married to a material girl.' Kuber is careful to not break the long lost friendship with Prahlad, that he has barely had a thin chance to recover.

Prahlad observes Kuber's stuttering, but for want of clarity, ignores his self dialogue as always. Kuber Savla is known to his friends to be a schizophrenic, so they each keep a safe distance. Emotionally as well.

It isolates Kuber even in their company.

Kuber is known to talk a lot to himself, he can be angry and aggressive at the same time, but he tries to keep his manners in public.

Sarkaar interjects, 'Both you Americans ruined our friendships, bringing business and money into everything. Let us try to have some peace at the resting place for Sid with a quiet prayer and a simple *sattvik* meal together.'

'You just want your deep fried potatoes you pygmy.' grumbles Kuber

'Oh why did we set out together? Looks like it was a bad idea!' cries out Yug. He places his hand on his forehead.

Sarkaar tries to build some consensus. 'Why don't we play a word game? Full life has passed us by, like these sceneries outside the window.'

'We have left school years back, why don't you move forward – you gunny bag!' A guffawing Kuber scorches Sarkaar again.

Sarkaar knows the reference to his body, yet he lets it pass, knowing his current fitness is better than Kuber, he does not wish to prove a point.

'Prahlad are you up for it?' Sarkaar knows that Yug will follow Prahlad so he looks at him next.

'Let's do it Sarkaar *Bhai*,' says Prahald.

'Let each one of us, list down the habits we love and hate, of any of our friends, not anyone in specific? Okay?' asks Sarkaar innocently.

There is some fresh air and thinking in the compartment. All the friends fall silent and apply their minds.

'I do not like your childish games Sarkaar. And I will answer specifically. Prahlad thinks he is the most intelligent of us all, while Yug is foolish to spend so much time behind family. There you go, all three done.' Kuber is pleased with himself, for having finished first.

'Yug baba,' interjects Sarkaar, before anyone tries to hurt Kuber back 'Try to keep it general.'

'You seem to be acting like Som Baaba yourself!' answers Kuber instead.

'Friends should not manipulate.' speaks out Yug looking toward Kuber, who turns a bit scarlet red behind his ears. 'All of us, had elder sisters when we grew up in our formative years and during our career rise. Each one did what he could, to help them. We did not use them as an excuse to alter the behaviour of our friends, or gyp them.'

Kuber looks out of the window. Lush green fields pass by, with coconut trees lining the periphery of all the fields. His longish hair fly and curl behind his neck.

'Friends I love, are those that have done things together and not wanted anything out of it. A good friend is one who wants to be with you in time and space. That's what I love in a friend. There is nothing to hate or dislike, if a friend is not friendly, then he is merely not a friend.' speaks Prahlad.

'And swindlers are surely not friends.' he ends conclusively.

Yug laps it all up and looks up to Prahlad as he always has and nods his head in agreement. 'A friend shows in his deeds, what a friend he is.' Yug is happy after his words come out right.

'Definitely, in deeds. Indeed.' says Sarkaar. 'None of us spoke as freely, when all five of us were there. I wish we had.' He looks toward Yug.

Sarkaar continues, 'Definitely Sid was born that way. Perhaps also raised that way. The biggest fact is he did not allow the establishment, or the environment or what happened to him, to sway him away from his own path. He had *Sattva gun, he believed in Sattvikta*. He was devoid of Rajas and Tamas. Neither over ambitious in activity nor lethargic of mind.'

Sarkaar after a gap, 'He treated people based on how they treated other friends, not how they treated him. He also saw to it, that there was never any unfairness between any one of us to another, but we all let him down.'

Som Sarkaar falls into the sadness trap himself that he had set out to avoid.

There is an uncomfortable silence, and Kuber is visibly upset with his companions. 'Why care so much...' he trails off, looking out of the window and turns his face away from the rest of them.

He continues his mumbo-jumbo to himself, as the train continues it's journey.

Ψ

It appears as if the quotient of time between each of the friends has paused and nothing has changed since Matheran.

All of them see each other, as if they are on the train journey for their school picnic to Matheran. They have canvas school bags on their bags, with wrinkled skin on their bodies. United in space and time, yet separate in spirit.

Neither has forgotten, leave aside forgiven. They have all aged so much, yet not gotten wiser.

Sarkaar's *drishti* imagines, as if he can see Sid in front of him; seated in the same *bogey of the train of thought*, open his tiffin. His dear friend feeds him a rice idli.

At first tears roll down his eyes as Sarkaar smiles like the child Som Sarkaar. They both look into each others vision. It rejuvenates Sarkaar. He can see ahead in Goa what Sid can see. Sarkaar's tears finally dry up, as he clears his illusion.

Sid gives him an expressive, 'let go' instruction, batting his eyelids with a soft plea. Sarkaar understands that he has to let go, looking into Sid's eyes he can remember all the meals they have eaten together.

Ψ

Sarkaar finally speaks up, 'Those who hurt you, have to be avoided Prahald!'

'You are right Som Bhai,' replies Yug. He implies taking a stand without looking at Kuber.

'The material is all immaterial.' chimes Prahlad, even after thirty years, he repeats himself like a stuck alarm clock.

'You would not feel that, if it was you he back-stabbed.' says Sarkaar about Kuber.

'He did Som, he did, many times. I agree, Sid never did.' Prahlad maintains the air of the more snobbish, the more intellectual and shuts out any further debate on the topic of their friendships.

As Kuber has kept gazing out, through the fields blankly, he remembers old memories from somewhere. Images of Portuguese news and talk in a Goan village come to him from as if nowhere and no one in specific from the fields.

He believes he can hear the chatter of Sid's conversations with him, and someone else. His sense of hearing is lost to the compartment of the train and he is oblivious to the talks of Som, Yug and Prahlad, who appear to be whispering to him.

Kuber has zoned out, his audibility and sense of hearing, smell and vision is lost momentarily.

'They think, they are the intellectuals, the Mr. Know it alls.' He mutters to himself. 'Rekha and Joanna would slay them, my mother would mock them, and I am sure my father would have crushed them, if they were his sons.'

Kuber's muttering is visible, and the friends fear a schizophrenic attack of aggression and agitation.

Just in time, Kuber turns toward them and shouts aloud, 'Monkey Island!!!'

Sarkaar jumps out of his skin, Prahald jumps off his seat, while Yug falls backwards as much due to age, as much as the train coming to a halt.

Kuber aggressively asks them all, 'If you all know so much about Goa, why don't you tell me, why did the Indian army have to be sent in? We had to throw the Portuguese out. Do you know that? They burnt the bridges down as they were leaving. Anything new that has to come, comes at the cost of destroying the past. In the same way, I had to build the hotel on the land we secured for the deal. Sid is gone, he is the past. He is the past for all four of us. Move ahead guys, he too wanted the hotel eventually.'

Yug speaks his truthful self, trying softly in Prahlad ears, but is loud enough to be heard across the entire compartment, 'There he sulks into his lies again. How can a person live a lie?'

Sarkaar breaks into a wry smile. Yet he keeps quiet initially and awaits his turn patiently. 'Are you defending the Portuguese Kuber? Would you be happier if they were running Goa? Why did the people of Goa ask for a plebiscite even before 1961? The Portuguese in Portugal disliked their own dictator, Salazaar. Look it up in history, he wanted his soldiers and sailors to burn everything down, '*not to leave stone on stone.*' were his orders, *Just destroy everything*. That is what you have done Kuber.'

Sarkaar looks at Prahlad next, expecting him to say something, and sit back upright.

Prahlad takes the hint given by Sarkaar, and breaks in weakly, 'You have destroyed whatever little our friendship stood for, by concealing your lies. We know the land belonged to Sid's forefathers and mother. You made him sign it off to you. I know everything from Rekha and your own sister. Why do you lie?'

'She is Schizophrenic, you believe her?' retorts Kuber.

'Oh, is she?' claims Yug and Prahlad in unison knowing fully well Kuber's own mental health condition.

'I am tired of references to Sid, whether he is there or not there.' shouts Kuber in an animated way. 'I am tired of him following us around wherever I go. In reference, in topics, in habits, in ideals, in intelligence, in, in...'

'Everything.' says Yug flatly. 'Initially I used to miss being part of your plans with Sid, but later I realized Sid alone bore the brunt of your foolish wisdoms. In the garb of today's Kalyug, and what works and what does not in you building your hotel, you did leave Sid behind, and out of it. He did everything with you and for you, fair and square.'

'Fair enough it was, otherwise Sid himself would have walked out of it, knowing his honesty and Kuber's scruples,' laughs Kuber, at himself.

'Well Kuber, whatever you did to me was forgiven, because I recovered. Yet what you did to Sid, was not fair. He was always there for you. The fact that you hid other '*gapplas*' you did was not enough. He never would have recovered to see, that you never improved yourself.' says Prahlad

Prahlad continues to reprimand, 'You removed him and Simi from your own company, for your lone consumption. What will you do with all this money? His family will never forgive you.' Prahlad sounds the death knell to their conversations and all four of them fall into a silent disquiet.

It is all immaterial.

It makes not much difference to Kuber, who ignores the diatribe. He now understands that the three of them are there, more to commemorate their pal Sid, rather than congratulate him for the opening of his fifth hotel in Goa.

The miser he is, he has bought only his own ticket to travel, and they have spent on their own. There is no need to leave any money to Rekha or Joanna so he really does not care, as they are no longer in his life since the past two decades.

Kuber continues to look out of the train, and again finds it very strange that the entire scenery looks very similar to him.

A deep sense of deja-vu overcomes him. He says more to himself, 'I have some unfinished business in Goa, something I have left still to do, it is pulling me back inside.'

He had never shared the secret of Sid's death. It had been their pact, which only the two of them knew.

After all, it was an offer, Sid could never refuse. It was connected to their past. To the Ra-Ro lives of Ray and Roy.

The desire to soar, the desire to fly.

Off the cliff...

26. Alliteration

A figure of speech using the same letter or sound at the beginning of words that are close together.

Illustration:

Endure the betrayl of 'false friends.'

26. Nightmare

That night when they reached Goa, Kuber sleeps in his own room. The night light dimly illuminates the tea and beverage area, while the ajar door of his room casts long shadows till the curtains.

'Why is the door not shut? Why is it open?' he mutters to his strutting self. His hip pointed outward on one side, his gait like a chimpanzee.

He has forgotten he has his friends with him in other rooms facing the beach. His room faces the main street on the other side.

He has kept the room curtains entirely closed, since he has eaten an early dinner in his bath robe, and slung into bed with it on. He worries about the morning sun. He prefers darkness in the morning, though he does not recollect why.

It is because he ends up sleeping with disturbance every night.

His next morning attire is on the study table chair. 'It hangs on the chair as loosely as the clothes will hang on my bony body tomorrow' he thinks.

He brushes his beard, staring in the mirror over the study table with his hands. He walks up and down on each of his legs, as if they were his hind legs, walking with each foot aside each other, Chaplinesque like.

'Am I the tramp? Am I the ape? Who came out of the cave?'

All the self talk is tiring. He has spoken not much on the train, except his self-muttering. He is tired of having spoken so much to himself since noon. The hotel room door has someone knocking.

He ignores the newspaper on the bed, which has Charlie Chaplin's photo and his death anniversary being celebrated by his fans. 'He was 88, he was 88...' he repeats to himself, ' I am just 78, going to be 79' he mutters.

He opens the room door that was left ajar, to find a butler outside. 'Your medication sir, as suggested by your doctor.'

The entire hotel staff knows of his condition. The chosen butler for the night is a tall bony dark skinned Goan, who looks as old as Kuber himself. It appears that he is staring at a mirror reflection of himself, and the reflection is handing him the tablet.

Kuber feels zonked and wonky.

'Oh yes, yes.' Kuber picks up the tablet, and with shaky hands, the glass of water. Kuber glug-glugs the water down his throat. The old butler looks at him suggestively to keep the glass back on the tray, and looks toward it.

Kuber thinks for a few seconds, till his reflection in the mirror dies out, and the butler becomes visible.

'Yes, yes, you f'cker! Get lost.' Kuber slams the door shut on the butler's face.

'That is why it was open. The door.' He walks back on the soft carpet, toward the curtains.

He looks at the array of bottles of beer, and the half empty bottle of Romonov Vodka on the study table. He pinches a neat peg directly from the bottle and snarls at his own reflection in the mirror.

'No hallucinations please. Please. Get myself some sleep.' A chimpanzee looks back at him from the mirror, and nods negatively, as would an ape saying yes.

It is as confusing to Kuber, as his state of mind. He strokes his beard disbelievingly.

Hours pass, and Kuber is slowly walking the width of the room like a tired monkey carrying his 'going bananas' load. 'Colva, Benaulim, Siolim, Colva, Benaulim, Siolim,...' he repeats again and again to himself.

He stops to view his reflection before the mirror each time, strokes his beard again, and then waits on the chimpanzee in the mirror to negate his sleeping plea.

He then continues the walk.

In the middle of this night stroll in the room, there is a noise outside the balcony sliding doors. Kuber can hear a few dogs bark. One dog whines and growls at the same time from a distance. The cries get louder, and more dogs join the party, as if calling out for their owners to feed them.

Kuber first plops himself on the bed. The growls outside continue.

He again bravely gets up from the bed, more than a bit stressed, as much as the dogs. He is himself now whining involuntarily.

Kuber in his half-sleep, half-drunk status, partly realizes that there is no chimpanzee in the mirror now. He can hear himself imitating the dogs noise, as if answering them, but he cannot stop himself.

He gets up to look at the mirror. An aged white beard Kuber stares back at him.

'Ah, the chimp has gone.' he says to himself.

As he leans against the balcony doors himself, he continues the whining. So do the dogs outside his room window, sort of replying to him. He recollects with a smile, that the same is a game he plays every night with them.

Kuber Savla is now terrified, and wonders, if the spirit of some dog has entered him. He flicks on both the table and study lamps of his room.

He looks at his reflection in the dressing mirror. He gimmicks grimacing his teeth as a dog would. Saliva drips out of his mouth.

There is a thud in the balcony and the glass panes of the sliding doors rattle. A swoosh noise comes from in between the balcony doors, caused by the cracks allowing the wind to rustle the thin curtains a fair bit.

There seems to be some external force on the balcony outside, its body outline frame visible through the curtains and glass panes on the door.

Kuber is now petrified. He again attempts to growl at the mirror, hoping to feel energized.

However, his hair stand on end at the nape of his neck and his back; a vibration going down his vertebrae down to his lower back.

The gap between the curtains part and get wider with the air through the crack of the doors from outside. He can see the image of Sid, as if standing with a parachute still strapped on his back. Sid looks at him in the eye.

The dogs begin to whine again.

Kuber cannot look him in the eye. He looks back at the study desk mirror, to see if the chimpanzee is there. He can only snarl like a dog himself. He is now fully gripped with the fear he feels inside his guts.

The barking gets louder and louder outside. It gradually gets so loud, as if it is coming from his room, so Kuber walks away from the balcony backward. He collides against his bathroom door which opens inward.

Stepping backwards into the toilet, he notices shaving foam and a razor ready on his bathroom slab. He feels his beard again now realizing that he has delayed his shave this evening too.

He remembers the butler who gave him the tablet to have placed it there.

He splashes water on his face, and takes a piddle. He is now running scared in his toilet, and is about to turn, when he hears the bath tub curtain rustle, and a hand come out from behind.

It is that of a dead Sid, with blood all over his face, offering a hand shake.

Kuber shouts out aloud a huge shrieking scream, 'Noooooooooooo...' and runs out of the toilet.

The dogs begin to bark again loudly. Some whine, some snarl, some bark in breaks. He can hear over five different kinds of dog menace, and can imagine the ruckus they create below his balcony room.

He had chosen the road facing room and given his friends the beach facing rooms the previous evening, ignoring the strays patrolling on the road outside the lobby facing street.

He ducks under his pillow, praying to himself.

'It is just a figment of your imagination.' comes the voice of Sid, as if being relayed on the ropes and harness of the parachute outside on the balcony.

Kuber can imagine, the parachute ropes dripping in red blood have caused a pool of water, sand, and red beer like foam outside on the balcony. His room gradually merges into the beach and waves collide against Kuber's bed on the wet sandy beach. He gets up to feel the water lapping his bed and places his feet on the wet carpet. He gets up from his bed, to get pulled back by the parachute ropes that are plugged into his ears.

Kuber is deep into his nightmare. Hours pass. Eventually at early dawn he finds himself on the floor of his hotel room dry carpet, under the study table.

His feet are sweaty, balmy in the humid non air-conditioned space. 'Shall I go to the toilet?' he asks himself.

Remembering the nightmare, where he finds Sid in the balcony and the tub, he convinces himself to go back to sleep with layers of the sheet and blanket wrapped around himself.

There is blood pounding inside his head, and he concentrates to hear any barks. There is silence. He remains crouched under the writing table of the room over his head.

'As if that will protect you?' he hears Sid's voice. There are noisy thuds in the balcony of the hotel room again. Shivering in fear, Kuber closes his eyes tightly, wraps the hotel sheets around his head to cut off his ears, and forces himself to sleep again.

Kuber wakes up eventually at noon, to find three coconuts and a large part of two stalks of palm tree branches resting on his balcony. '*Perhaps this was thudding and collapsing on my window panes and sliding doors,*' he whispers.

He looks out through the glass doors, to find any stray dogs and observes no sign of human life. He pinches himself walking to the toilet and places his hands under hot water in the sink, to know fully well that he is entirely awake.

He observes the shaving foam on his hotel toilet mirror, having made a crying smiley.

He hurriedly takes out toilet paper and wipes the foam off the mirror. He throws the trash into the commode.

The water runs in the toilet for an hour, as Kuber shaves slowly, and keeps the tub curtains aside. He continues to look at the mirror ahead of himself, to check on reflections behind.

There is so much shaving foam on his face, and his hands, that Kuber is initially unable to shave on one side, as he over-shaves the same side repeatedly giving himself a knick and few cuts, below his side-locks.

Little does he know, friendly ghosts don't show up in the mirror in the morning.

They show up only at night. They creep up on your sub-conscience. They appear when you are in your sleep to haunt you, like whining loyal dogs.

After shaving, Kuber keeps a close record of his country revolver gun, checking on it every few minutes in his travel knapsack bag.

He shifts it from the bag, to his suitcase. Then again into his suit inner pocket.

He cannot decide a safe and secure place for it. It is a gift from his Mumbai connections with the underworld. He cannot decide for whose protection he has kept it. His own, or for defence against an unseen unknown enemy. It has turned him into a hostile yet fearful person.

This fear is of the unknown, the unseen, it has started driving him crazy.

He questions himself during his sane hours, 'Who really am I fearful of? Not the law of the land, not the friend who can squeal on me, Sid is gone!' His hotels are running on the finances that he had got from Rekha and Sid.

He cannot seem to forget that. It is turning him mad.

Every morning, he forgets he is diagnosed as a schizophrenic patient. He remembers a bit of the nightmare. Either the dogs part, or the chimpanzee part.

He keeps staring at mirrors.

He is afraid of what it may reflect.

To live with so much of fear, so much of hallucination becomes difficult. It needs silencing the mind, yet he never gets more than a few hours of sleep, despite the drinks.

So the nightmares continue.

His meds and his alcoholism numbs his senses for a few hours of sleep under the study tables of different rooms every night.

Every night the butler follows him into different rooms for his medication, but finds him drunk and confused before he consumes his meds.

He trusts only himself. Even at the age of nearly 79.

Kuber has to work hard to stay sober. True to himself. He meanders in that too. He tells himself to believe incorrect things, to erase the past.

He tries to find joy in happenstance, in the Goan way of life, but the people are as unconnected to him, as they were to Portugal.

The tourism is very seasonal, and people tend to holiday during select months of the year. The hotel he runs has low traffic for over ten months of a year. Very few new people migrate in fits and bursts toward the end of the year, and Kuber fails to recognize them next year.

His various trips to the place, has not made him feel any sense of belonging. He waits for the circumstances to change, as if luck will just happen by chance. He has neither succeeded nor failed.

The six hotels he has built, stand. But he himself stands alone.

He remembers via reading his notes in his laptop bag every day, that he owns six hotels. By late night he forgets one or two, due to his state of mind.

He gets out of his room every morning, and instructs the valet of his hotel, to drive him to any one of the other hotels.

The same acts repeat there; he drinks himself silly, consumes tablets more than food, and hallucinates. This morning the valet tells him to wait for his friends and Mr. Vaz, who has offered to drive them to "THE SERENITY" hotel behind Palolem beach, near Sid's cliff.

'Ah Palolem! I remember now, Colva, Benaulim, Siolim and Palolem.' He struggles to remember the other two at Candolim and Varca.

He waits silently, till his friends come down. He has forgotten the previous day's train journey.

All he can remember, again and again, is Sid, with a parachute.

'Or is it Auntie Tia's *porga*, Ray?' he thinks to himself in the waiting car.

PART – 4.

The Bonhomie

27. Euphemism

A figure of speech, that speaks indirectly to convey something difficult or embarassing.

Illustration:
Sid's soul hangs around at the private aircraft hangar...

(Signifying death of human form)

27. Soul Searching
(a day before)

Sid's soul had been hanging around at the private aircraft hangar in Goa's Dabolim International Airport. He could hear the train chugging into the station like it had the last time his human form took the journey from Mumbai to Goa; he was missing Simi today, as much as he was on that train.

Sid's soul, hanging at the hangar, looks up at the cloud, to hear the conversation of his friends in the train, it downloads to his spirit quite fast, as the train has slowed down upon entering Goa.

'Still sparring and warring after so many years. They never grow up.'

The private hangar cohabits the space with his child hood big buddy Dinshaw. Both of them jump off the wings of the private aircraft, making the aircraft lighter by two more soulful passengers, albeit light ones.

Sid's ghost sporting his trade mark goggles and blue hat walks along with that of his ex-friend's, his arm around Dinshaw's shoulder. 'DinDin, you looking much slimmer man, since you grew your handle-bar moustache.'

'Advantage of being a ghost my pal, no need to shave, no need to loose any more weight. Everyone is not as light and formless as you were when you were alive. Also you get to sport and remain in the last look you sported before you die. I am so happy I was in a white Kurta Pyjaama, and empty stomach the day I got my attack. I simply fell off the chair, when your son called to speak to me. It sounded so, so,... much like you.'

'Yeah he does, he talks like me, but does not walk like me,' says Sid. 'By the way, you look like a cool hippy of the 1970's. You didn't need to shave then too, if only you had grown up then.'

'The stroke was fatal man, I guess I spent too much time, thinking too much. Thinking about our last Goa trip, our misadventure. Not every one can be ahead of their times like you, you lived well, beat me at it, early come, early go. This formless living, hearing the clouds, breathing the rain, watching over the blue sea. You led me to the right path. Now here I am, best place to be in the world. Goa... aaaah.......Goaaaaah !'

Dinshaw takes a deep breath, 'Transported to this hangar with you. Could you not have selected a more comfortable spot?'

Both the friends, pre-occupied by different things, saying many different things, dime a dozen, yet like when they were alive in human form, they understand each other completely.

'It downloads faster here from the clouds, whether *Mumbaikars* travel by train or air, I can hear them come. Hear them go. You would sing, Go to Goa, Go to Goa...'

'Goa meri hai.' responds Dinshaw.

'The blue sea, watching waves break, people walking out of the church, trying. Trying to live, trying to pray. Not all are sinners, sure some are. Not all are booze bummers, many are. Not all are lazy people, few are.'

Dinshaw speaks, 'True blue brother, true blue. I just hope, the sun does not fall from the sky, the clouds do not disappear, the rain stops falling, the sand stuck like glue. I dunno...I smell some trouble brewing in Goa.'

'Why do you always dream of an apocalypse? Pessimism also has its expiry limits in Goa. Don't wear it on your sleeve. You are a Spook now, me a Ghost. What can't hurt us, will not bite us.'

'Ah...formless living...if only we could reverse age and live again.' Dinshaw wants another life. Sid delays him and keeps him hanging at the hangar every night

Sid guides, 'You want to reincarnate? For that you have to let things happen, not stop them from happening. Your past allows you to make just one choice. So choose the next womb carefully. Rationality over Emotionality.'

Dinshaw emotes, 'Always difficult for me, the world always called me mental, sentimental.'

'Well, the world we lived in was outside Goa; not very normal, for the times we came from. Not everyone was normal, some were. Not everyone was nice, some were.'

Dinshaw speaks, 'You should say, everyone was mostly poor, bad or corrupt.'

Sid leads again, 'Ssh...*the GodMan* is listening, he will bless us for a re-birth. Be careful what you say, you will be born with that nature again, face the same circumstances again.'

Dinshaw carefully, and softly, 'How frustrating! Yet, now I know from you, it is the way of the universe. We forgot about that on Bombay's Earth.'

'Our wireless speeds and transfer on Goan Blue Bop network is quick. No complaints there I hope Dinshaw?'

'Well, the lesser said about that. I rather go on living here, it is a more immediate form of entertainment, from a breaking news or gossip point of view. No need to buy cinema tickets, travel, eat drink or make merry. Just float from the hangar with the clouds, to the beaches, surf with the sea, break wind with the wind-surfers, ride a boat on the shoulder of a young teenage kid.' Dinshaw has rattled off the 'Goa meri hai...' menu from his head.

'Ah, now you talking! Just that we lack more company.' cribs Sid. 'And I say that in a good way, for both of us. We need newer topics, till we are suddenly re-born again.'

'Let us be judicious, and not say the wrong things that *the GodMan* hears.'

Dinshaw changes track, 'I guess you still waiting for Simi? She was always happier in Mumbai.'

'You don't know, you don't say.' replies Sid. 'She was happy anywhere, when she was with me. I used to believe she was happy anywhere at all, but now, from up here, and download from the cloud, I see her to be unhappy, despite travelling to Goa. Despite having all the money. Waiting to see her up here, based on which I will choose, to remain unborn, or take a re-birth.'

'Really, you willing to go through it all again?? You cheat, you just waiting for your lady love Simi.' Dinshaw perplexed, to understand what really does Sid want, and figure out his own desire. 'Should I follow my friend, or charter my own path?'

Sid, proposes to explain, 'If you see carefully, what does living give us as a human, that we can't do from up here? We can fly about without paying airfare, we can't be seen, though we can watch all the ladies sun-bathing at the beach and at the pools all over Goa.'

'Hmm, true that. True blue.' replies Dinshaw.

'We don't need food, so there is no issue with obesity or diabetes. Clean crisp air is good enough to carry us. The calm Arabian sea water to keep our vision, and help us to charter our course, and the green trees help us pull back at night, before sunrise and dawn. What more can you ask for?' claims Sid.

'Being a spook has it's perks,' Dinshaw is smiling again. 'No fun being human.'

Sid counsels, 'What will you do differently then if you are reborn? Again the cycle of school, teenage music, girls, more girls, some sport, marriage, kids, losing ageing parents, financial stress, then self ageing, and hopefully dying without an unpaid mortgage, debt, relationship disasters, disease, conflict, or controversy.

'Right!' Agrees Dinshaw. 'True blue. Goa meri hai...'

Sid continues, 'This formless living is more soulful, I rather remain a ghost that I am, and hope that Simi makes it too. Till then I have you around me, a good spook like you. Better than any friend on planet earth.'

Dinshaw seems unconvinced, 'Hmmm...Goa teri hai, Goa meri hai... I come to Goa, come to Goa, Goa meri hai.'

'You are looking for a dog's life, find yourself a bitch; you will be at the place and mercy of your future master,' suggests Sid.

Dinshaw with full concentration, is now on a mission, 'Well, I take a right turn at Benaulim. Looking for bitches my friend. And hopefully some bonhomie.'

Some friends, seek advice, some seek a path, some think differently, some still live as a good soul unlike an average human.

Dinshaw was all of the above and more, but he knew, the unconditional love a dog could give and receive.

He wanted that easy loving life that Goa had to offer, and yearned for more. He had been through sport, enjoyment, and a pure material existence, that it was all immaterial to him. 'I agreed with Prahlad many a time, before and after dying as a human.'

Their paths diverged. They would soon be missing at Palolem beach, where they would meet daily.

It is what happens, when you choose differently, the path less trodden.

You are on your own.

Sid in a serene tone, wished his friend well, 'See ya, on the other side, I turn left for Vaarca. I may just keep floating...looking for the real thing.'

28. Antithesis

A figure of speech, that places two completely contrasting ideas in juxtaposition.

Illustration:

The material, is immaterial.

28. Dinshaw's Day Off

Butterfly Island. A small cove, south of Palolem, it is an ideal spot for honeymooning couples. Young humans, in a different zone of their lives, rubbing their feet in the sand together, while butterflies swarm the hillocks going upwards from the beach.

The privacy at the beach is what couples in their swimsuits and trunks enjoy, away from the gaze of other tourists and holiday makers.

It was Dinshaw's reclusive place to rest his soul.

He could see some couples aiming to have sex eventually, and he hoped to size them up before, to choose his future family.

The couples had taken the boat ride from Palolem, and only strong swimmers were allowed on the boats due to the depth of the waters. Dinshaw had held back on this cloudy offer for rebirth as he enjoyed the free spirited life that South Goa had to offer.

It felt murky to be reincarnated again and have the power to choose. Like choose one's friends, one's own parents. It was the rare power that only he and Sid, the star angels of Goa had.

They had held back to take birth again, as their souls were carefree in Goa.

Once couples became parents, they behaved like rats.

Sid and Dinshaw were afraid, that they would join the rat race back in Mumbai or wheresoever in India the mating couples came from.

Often, Sid found a couple from the hills of Himachal and Dinshaw found families hailing from far away Rajasthan.

Then there were other things to consider, like the sport they played if any, the pre-existing disease or an elder sibling, like a domineering elder brother or a cranky younger sister. Or vice-versa.

Dinshaw and Sid went back to their free spirited lives often, wanting to play the solo act. Sid was also genuinely waiting for Simi, being the hopeless romantic between the two.

Dinshaw knew he had lost his mind in Mumbai, and left his body behind. He was elated it was all done and dusted in Mumbai, and all he had was his spirit.

He had enjoyed the equity in his bond with Sid, and he knew heart of heart, that they both had been charitable soft souls, not meant for the city of Bombay once it became Mumbai.

Corrupt, dirty, opportunistic, and fast paced that the city life was, Goa offered them the chance to not just look ahead for their future life, but to allow their soul to float the beaches they missed when they were alive in Mumbai.

It was the same opportunity for humans on holiday, but they went back to being rats.

They did not have bills to pay, nor houses to keep, nor wives to provide nor children to rear.

They waited on the ultimatum they knew the Gods from the clouds would give, to look for a finite time for rebirth, when India was at its epic moment in history, which looked like, now actually.

So NRI's were not an option, as were the rejected Russians and British tourists. The Americans had stopped coming. Pun intended. The Japanese too were an ageing race. So foreigners were also ruled out.

Yet, now they were as light as the breeze, and fleeting moments could be spent on a day off from angelic duty, flying like a butterfly. It was what gave Dinshaw the power to be who he was. Mainly spook, but the one day holiday to be like a human.

He took perch at the base of a coconut tree, gazing at the grass and bushes beyond. It reminded him of Sundays at Bandstand Bombay; on planet earth.

While enjoying his Goan paradise, Dinshaw watches a praying mantis come and sit safely in the centre of a bush close to his feet. It was surrounded by pretty patterned butterflies and tons of yellow ones that flew around the height of Dinshaw's head.

He took more inspiration from the butterflies, as he saw many collapse, fly away, and perish in seconds. The praying mantis looked at the butterflies who lost part of their wings at times if they collided too hard with the leaves of the bushes on the shore.

It appeared to Dinshaw, that the praying mantis like Sid's soul would say, 'Ttch, ttch.' Sid conserved his energy like the praying mantis, as he lacked venom.

Little light yellow sawdust flew off the wings of the butterflies, as they were yellower than the clean beach they bred on.

The praying mantis flies out in Dinshaw's direction, and lands on the bark of the coconut tree. It cannot sense or differentiate the direction of the sound that emanates from Dinshaw's light whistle.

The mantis sits in the praying position, as does Sid often. 'Sigh, I already miss my friend. Human tendencies do not leave the soul.'

Like the praying mantis, Sid knew, their chances of survival if they choose a healthy womb, are better than the butterflies. He has been stalling Dinshaw to avoid taking rebirth as a butterfly, for its span of life and impact is short.

Enamoured as he is, by the flitting butterfly species, Dinshaw does take his friend's advice. He observes with marvel in the green grass he basks, the praying position that the mantis takes, with its long front legs. It's a head turner with its two large compound eyes, that work together to decipher it's visual cues.

Dinshaw grumbles to himself, 'Yet to live like a butterfly and look like a mantis – with vision, agility and predatory skills would have been so ideal, why can we never get the full deal in life?' He takes off, as suddenly as the Praying mantis flies off too.

Dinshaw controls himself, and does not give up his soul, to become a beautiful butterfly in form. He gives up the butterfly birth option.

He floats ahead to find, a couple walking their pet Spitz. 'Oh the life of a dog, one of amazing friendly loyalty, with not a care to provide, only to eat and wag one's tail at the master's discretion, like the mantis turns it's head on the butterflies.'

As his thoughts mix up between the choice of species and to avoid human form, he encounters on the beach, a lout, sleeping completely drunk and pissed in his shorts in the summer.

Dinshaw messages to the clouds, to increase the shade over that spot. 'Not that this man cares, but what a waste. He does not know where he is. What is the point of being alive, if one is so unconscious?'

He watches two young children, build a massive sand castle with much concentration. Their sand pails, filled with wet sand, carefully upturned by them, their tongues tightly held over their upper lips, as their slippery fingers let loose the bucketful of sand, They use their small wet hands to shape the castle better, and then layback to admire it.

Their parents come and pass them some ice-cream on sticks.

'Oh there is hope in the world, if we can be young at heart again, and again, till forever. Rarely do kids do any wrong, mischievous souls, seeking pleasure and licking their ice-cream dollies.'

The sister is enjoying her choco-bar while the brother is licking with speed, the red dripping strawberry duet.

Their slippers upturned, their wet beach towels, lying around them in the sand, their carefree spirit, digging and toiling away, to make their sandy homes on the beach. The proverbial human dream is inculcated subconsciously as a child. 'Stay young at heart my friend, you are right Sid, even just our spirits need that without re-birth.'

He looks toward their parents, on the side going towards the upper beach area. They lie down with their legs criss-crossing, immersed with both their feet inside the sand. They sit with their bums on a bedsheet with towels around their wet shoulders.

'In peak of their youth, adulthood, the man smokes his cigar. This wretched smell floats and disturbs me.' Dinshaw blows strongly at the wind, and the cigar drops.

The wife likes it that her husband has lost his thick roll of tobacco. She laughs at the husband hysterically, who gazes at her angrily, and is about to growl yet holds back his aggression. He looks at the cigar losing it's spark in the wet sand, and is about to pull out his feet from under the sand. His wife stops him, placing her hand on his knee.

She looks at him sweetly, and points in the direction of the children. His look softens. He overcomes the loss of his cigar, for the higher pleasure to simply gawk at his wife, wet, in the sultry weather her hair crossing over her forehead like a fishing net.

Around her head, is the setting sun, and in the back-drop - the boat they had taken to the beach from Palolem.

The man can hear his children gurgle in pleasure as their two stacks of sand pails stand the wind and complete the back portion of their palace.

Happy in their make-believe world, the children's exuberance rubs off on their father; he inhales a deep breath of salty beach air. He feels the pride of having fathered his two children. He admires his wife again, who now also looks to oversee her children.

The husband feels relaxed, and colour returns to his face.

His wife mocks him sweetly with her frowned nose. He gesticulates at her to head back to the room for some action.

She points at the children and reminds him, that there is the night, and the moon is yet to shine after the evening. 'There is time...' she mouths, '...we still have a few days.'

He acts out an encore rolling his hands, and copying her curves. 'My dear, this is the best phase of my life...'

Ψ

'Aah! You got it pal, you got it.' exclaims Dinshaw to himself.

'The cigar, the material was immaterial. What you have is everything under the sun and clouds, before the deep waters, with the docked boat watching your back, Enjoy this moment, for this is life at it's fullest.

You don't know when it will return, and by the time you come back here again, your wife will be older, you would be grumpier, your children would have left home and you can then - have your cigar and smoke it from your butt if you wish! I will surely not be here, to blow it out of your hands. No one in your family will stop you or be there to care and tell you anything, so you better hold on to this moment.

Hold on to it, hold on to it! Just like the transcendental momentary beauty of the butterflies flying away like saw dust at the back of the beach, by the bushes near the grass by the side of the coconut tree. My human friend, you have no idea of beauty and life. It *is the most beautiful phase* of your life!'

Ψ

Sid sends him a message via the clouds. 'Yug has been gambling at the Casino at Panjim, Prahlad has spent some quality time with his daughter, taking her to the St. Sebastien Church. Sarkaar has walked and walked all over South Goa's village as if to practice for a walkathon. Only Kuber has lived it up, drinking late into the evening as always, at Zeebop. I worry for him. He planned to walk back along the beach late at night.'

'You are mad,' replies Dinshaw.

'Well, he used to say during our Goa trip, *you are like my brother*. I am bound to worry,' says Sid with deep human emotion and feeling, as if it was just yesterday that they were in college. Alive.

'He was not even your friend,' responds Dinshaw. 'Oh how boring Sid for you looking out like an angel. You have taken the task too seriously. I am having a splendid day. No doubt. You are right, it is the vision of a praying mantis, and living in the moment like a butterfly.'

Sid reminiscing, 'We used to have *phone a friend*, in a popular game show contest on television, when we were alive. We used to refer to it in college when our syllabus notes were missing after cyclostyling.'

'Xerox you mean, copying! That's what friends did. In real life, it was more like, fool a friend.' laughed back Dinshsaw.

Sid tries to keep his tone soft, and not blame, 'I thought you had gone looking for a mother. Till we find one, we have to do our angelic jobs!'

'I found mother nature.' says Dinshaw rather simply. 'Yet I know what you mean, we have to use our power judiciously.'

'Enough of waiting to see the life-guard and the fishermen of Palolem choose their wives. These buggers are never gonna get married, leave aside fornicate to have children...' says Sid, 'Time is running out for us.'

'They will Sid, they will, have the patience, and the eyes of your Praying Mantis. And as you say, pray....we will find the Goans to stay back in Goa.'

'You sure Sir Dinshaw?'

'On the conscience of my spirit soul, I am sure my Sir Sid.'

'Okay, Goa it is then. Let's wait. In the meantime, I can look out for my friends.'

The clouds have parted, and the sultry weather turns sunnier.

29. Metaphor

A figure of speech, in which a word or phrase is applied to an object or action to make a comparison, or <u>explain an idea</u>.

Illustration:
Sid has relied on that in this formless living, for he has the life of an angel.

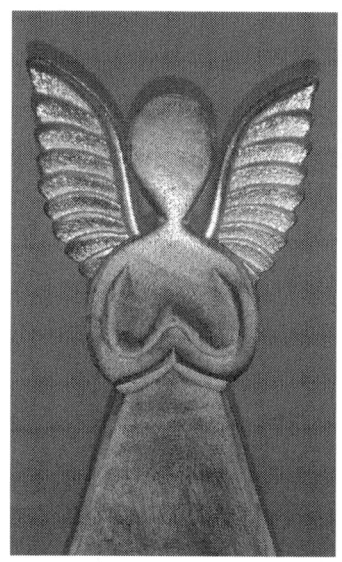

29. Friendly Angelic Ghost

Dinshaw and Sid look at each other. They are back at Palolem beach the next day, having not found their respective wombs.

Perhaps the humid summer heat, kept dogs and humans at bay; avoiding sex, and enjoying sun-bathing or the local feni.

The bright sun was out again, unnoticed by the other four. The previous evening's cool Goa rainy breeze was unfelt, not experienced by either of the four of them.

Today was completely another day for Prahlad, Yug, Kuber and Som Sarkaar.

Coming from Mumbai, the only thing common remaining between the four of them, is that they each had money and tensions on their mind.

Aged and bent backs, they had no other thing in common.

Sid had kept track of the trains ending at Madgaon station every day over the years. He knew fully well, that his friends will take the rail tracks, and not the air route.

He looks for international passengers at the airport, only to see if he can merge their DNA and love interests, with someone at Vaarca Beach, for his own conception. He has remained unsuccessful. They both were happy that they were given an intermediate angelic form, so are picky and in no hurry.

The were overjoyed before entering heaven to not have formed into ghouls, who hung around grave yards, feeding off the energy from the many buried bad sinners graves in Goa.

Being a ghoul, was worse than being the suffering humans on earth or even cannibals. It was a form of formless transitory re-birth that was a punishment from the universe and the GodMan.

You fed on the little flesh and blood from the new dug graves and the negative vibrations from older graves, to get a rebirth as a pig, an animal that fed on just about anything. Or you were reborn an evil consuming human pig, to devil on earth parents. The sort who wrecked havoc within families and friends.

So, they hang around the repair and refuelling hangar of private aircrafts. They play imaginary games over the aeroplane wings, flying kites and killing old wasps by blowing them into the engines.

Yet Sid spends the maximum holiday time with Dinshaw.

'These fellows still do not understand death, and how close they are to it.' Dinshaw guffaws to Sid. Dinshaw has been blessed with a futuristic vision that tells him about lives ahead by twelve hours. Sid has relied on that in this formless living, to stay safe, and keep Dinshaw out of trouble as well.

They conspire, to inspire each other. Theirs is a pact of real bonhomie. So that day they reunite their angelic forces to accompany their earth friends.

Sid and Dinshaw, take their seat on the carrier loaded over the roof of the Minnova MUV as the aged friends leave their friend's hotel to go find the spot, where Sid had fallen off the cliff.

Kuber tries to break the ice again, 'So which of you plans to invest in my company? You can buy a hotel room, any one from the ninety rooms. It is for life, like a time share. It will guarantee you this holiday for ten days a year for life. Live your golden years, at Serenity Hotels – a resort by Kuber Savla.'

'How many years of life do we have left living you clown?' fires Sarkaar.

Prahlad interjects, 'I am happier in America, so no chance of me moving to Goa; let's get the homage to Sid done and get out of here.'

Yug intercepts Prahlad, and gets him back to the Goa site, 'Simi had said she will call from the airport, but she hasn't called yet. She said she will see us directly at the spot behind Palolem Beach.'

Sid's ears perk up. On the name of Simi.

The four of his friends keep bickering, and continue to argue their respective point of views.

Som Sarkaar stops talking much, as he realizes he is outnumbered with Prahald and Yug, forming their own comfort zones. He knows, that Kuber is only after money, which he has none to offer.

He learns that well from Prahlad. Yug is too tight fisted for even Kuber to make a dent into his savings. Besides, Yug is not for relaxing and time shares. He plays the stock market well out of Mumbai, and has heaps invested there, with the index tipping over a three hundred thousand. Yug feels like a million bucks, despite his blood-pressure and back pain.

Prahlad has aching knees, it is only Sarkaar who still has good muscle mass and moves about freely, with his short arms and short legs, moving in a hare like manner.

The vulture that he is, Kuber has not forgotten his school days with all of them. Seated in the front seat of their taxi, his thoughts go back to Matheran.

As the car reaches a Y shape fork, with a blind curve bend on the road, a bus comes out of nowhere. It impacts their car head-on and climbs over the bonnet of their car at a high speed of 90 kilometres per hour.

They say life is short.

Yet you don't see death coming, unless it is upon you.

That is the thing about love and death, they both find you.

Ψ

Sid always called Dinshaw, for his magic powers to see ahead of time. In crisis too, he was the best friend to contact.

Especially when he desired a wish to come true. 'Save them if you can Dinshaw.' Sid always had some special requests.

Dinshaw tells him, 'Don't be partisan. Save the wish for our ex-wives from human life, or our ex-kids. You were the one who has endured a *bogey bonhomie* with these guys.'

Sid hoped his magical thinking had the genie effect on him.

The foolish optimist could never be the paranoid pessimist like Dinshaw, something that had saved Dinshaw from lots of trouble and bad luck.

'Sarkaar was never wrong, nor mean, nor competitive, nor egoistic. Just a bit silly and dependent. He was alone, unmarried till the end, that's all. Save him, move him in the car, we have 90 nanoseconds till they are all suspended in thin air inside the car.'

The fact was they both were gone from planet earth all together, but their spirit souls hungover and hovered around air-craft hangars and car carriers.

They were suspended atop coconut trees on both sides of the road, talking to each other, while their friends below remained suspended in pain, frozen in time and nano seconds. Few nano-seconds on the planet earth in human form, can be debated for hours between Ghosts and Spooks, to decide their fate.

Their friends had come to Goa unlike others who came to Goa for a different kind of spirit, and 'hangover.'

Ψ

'Dinshaw, we are okay being dead aren't we? Look at these fellows. Let them be. Save them. Move on, their families, folks and friends need them on planet earth.'

Dinshaw replies, 'Why don't we head toward the beach at Palolem, maybe Simi needs us there, while I can continue enjoying gaping at the lovely tourist ladies there. We wasted our youth on drinks, and these foolish friends of yours. Let's use our soul searching time well now.'

Dinshaw pauses, and Sid kindly acknowledges him, knowing that he cannot upset Dinshaw, who continues his tirade, 'They will not see us anymore now, two of them will head towards the graves as ghouls, eating up whatever is left of the other's dead body. So Sid what is the point?'

'Perhaps Sarkaar, even Yug could be reborn as regular humans. Let them be reborn as masseurs of Goa. Think about it. We will hear their chatter till we hang around here. For them to be re-born, they have to survive this.'

'They felt jealous when we were alive, with so many options to choose from, they were either busy with TV or porn.' proclaims Dinshaw.

Sid has first justified his pleas. Now he appeals harder, 'Those are hardly crimes these days Dinshaw. Come on, do it. The GodMan listens to you.'

Dinshaw knows, that the GodMan listens to him, 'Where was he, when you were planning to stupidly jump off the cliff.'

'Kuber had made me *an offer too good to refuse*. Perhaps the GodMan was busy saving other better souls, better lives.'

That was an understatement

'It was my dream, the cliff over-looked the misty seas, the salty air made me feel so heady. Vaz and Stanley had laid the trap so well, they had gotten me a suit, with wings, zipped over connecting my arms to my legs, like a webbed frog's hands. I could see a blazing trail of turtles below on the Palolem beach, it was a sight to behold. I took it as a sign.'

'With no harness, no safety belt?' says an amazed Dinshaw.

Sid goes on to clarify, 'Well, Kuber knew from Mumbai, that I had been disallowed to do bungee jumping. I would not jump out of an aircraft to try aerial diving, as Simi would not allow it. He had me here, and it was all planned and we had trained for it in Karjat and Matheran, close to his cousin's villa overlooking similar but smaller mountains.'

'You kept it a secret from us, from me, from Simi.' Dinshaw went into a sulk again. 'I had warned you off, as I always felt this man, this Kuber Savla, to be too keen to take risks.'

'It was fair enough, he made me sign the papers of the property before I jumped off the cliff, it was my own choice, I can only blame myself.' says Sid honestly.

Dinshaw disagrees, 'His intentions were always bogus. He was your bugbear, and weighing you down, his entire life. Like a leech.' Dinshaw was beyond conviction and Sid could see it was not working.

(Kuber, Som Sarkaar, Prahlad and Yug remain suspended in mid-air in their car below, in the two third period of the nano second.)

'Do what you can do Dinshaw. For all my friends.' And Sid left it at that. Sid was simply ghosting his friend Kuber Savla, for a very long time, till he came back into his life with the Goa dream.

Dinshaw was playing the Spooked friend he was. He was Sid's eternal devil's advocate.

'Sid lemme tell you again. Only a friend in deeds, is a friend indeed. Everything else, is just empty words and manipulation. If you can't hold them responsible, then it is what they call gaslighting down there on earth.'

'Indeed my friend, in deed, you are one such friend.' Sid smiles and sits atop the coconut tree, on the other side of the road, while he watches his friend Dinshaw intently, rubbing his hands in circles.

Dinshaw says, 'Those who are no longer in need, or in deed with us, are they no longer our friends? What of the good times, the bonhomie...of the past in this earlier life, of the past life?'

Sid puts in a word again, 'I still think for them, worry for them. They are lost souls. Perhaps what they suffered - was not just due to this life.'

Dinshaw is looking up at the clear sky for the cloud. He awaits his download and the command of the GodMan of the universe. 'If only she was a GodLady, she would have heard me faster, our boss G'Man is slow, whether on earth or in the universe, man just fails to multiplex.'

'When you can find fault in the GodMan, then why cry over a friend?' pat comes the rhetorical reply from Sid.

A booming voice interrupts their debate. 'Many orders in the pipeline Dinshaw. Here is my approval for three lives,' thunders the GodMan, and Dinshaw's palm branch shakes as he is surprised with the sudden revert and approval.

Ψ

Luckily humans could not see all this in Goa, or elsewhere, on how their lives were transacted. Otherwise living their day to day lives would be impossible, even outside hospitals.

Each of the Coconut trees, had these ghosts, ghouls and spooks in every lane in Goa, and they came out after sun-set. The clouds were more visible, and audible for the empowered souls in the evening.

Surprisingly the Portuguese had left none of their kind souls behind. It was really an Indian territory now...and Indian souls had to think about the European tourists too.

The front cabin of the car is crunched under the weight of the heavy tyres of the bus. Shreds of blunt glass are all over Kuber's body and all over his face.

The sun-block cover over the windshield, has come off, and hit the side of Kuber's left temple, from where he is bleeding profusely. The mirror glass from inside that has entered his right eye, while the steel wire from the sun-blocker has gone into his left ear. He seems barbecued into the windshield, with glass shreds sprinkled all over - like herbs and parmesan over a battered pizza. His hair, rolled up in long curls is as twisted as red pasta in red sauce, the blood all over his white shirt, turning it rouge like.

Sarkaar who is seated behind him, is magically saved, though trapped inside his seat belt cutting over his chubby chest, his eye-balls pop in front staring at the driver.

Driver Vaz's body is a mangled mess, resembling a heap of Chicken Xacuti. His Portuguese forefathers would have called him *chacuti*.

Prahlad recovers first, 'My leg is smashed, it is stuck under the driver's seat Yug. I can't feel my feet he exclaims, help me!'

Yug can hear a shrill bomb like squeak in his ears, as they ring non-stop. He cannot believe that the car he is seated in has got smashed. He stares at his OnePlus 18 cell phone, in his right hand, the screen of which is broken. He looks ahead diagonally to see the entangled mess that Kuber's body appears like a red lasagne, with red pizza sauce over coils of fusilli pasta. He cannot register, if he is mistaken from last night's Italian meal at the hotel.

He can't speak, as words fail to come off his mangled bitten tongue. Yug thinks, *'Or has it has all come down to this so soon? Is this The End?'*

He cannot hear Prahlad's words. It appears to Yug that he is shouting his pleas. Prahlad thinks he is being ignored by Yug, grimacing in pain.

Sarkaar is seated quietly, *'Is this all a bad dream? Why did I join this group? What brought me here? I had never seen Goa, but I had seen enough of these fools.'*

Sarkaar unstraps his safety belt, gets out of the car, and begins to walk away, slowly. Very slowly. Very very slowly.

'Walk, walk, walk is all I can do to get help.' Sarkaar does not carry a cell phone, and knows no one in that village. He decides to walk back to Serenity Hotels, leaving his friends there in the car.

Passengers from the bus begin to alight.

A passenger amongst them is Simi, in the shuttle service from the airport on way to Raj Exotica. She recognizes Yug and Prahlad in the back-seat, and cajoles the bus crew, and some of the passengers to help. She dials the local hospital and ambulance for help searching them on google.

'Like husband, like wife,' grins Dinshaw.

'The saying is like father, like son, she is her father's daughter. Resourceful, and strong in crisis. I usually used to crumble, ' accepts a happy Sid.

'Well your pillar of strength is here. Go about floating around her now for the next few days. Let me know when do I get to see you again?'

'Thanks DinDin, for saving Sarkaar,' says Sid. ' You are my favourite genie.'

'Yug will also make it, after the initial din settles down in his ears,' clarifies Dinshaw. 'Prahlad will also be let off with a small limp tomorrow. It is in the same leg that he had broken himself years back. They have idiosyncrasies, and are not idiots. They kept wrong company, that's all, not very different from you.'

Sid winks back gleefully.

'I could not save Kuber. The ManGod decided his destiny, and over ruled me. I know you would have wanted to protect him too. Frankly, it was long expected the way he was living life in the fast lane."

He is left reassured for the rest of his three friends, who have children and wives dependent on them.

Sid speaks ruefully, he is a bit glum, not really sad. 'Why do evil people meet bad ends?'

'There is space at the grave yard my friend.' Dinshaw floats away from the coconut trees, as a herd of monkeys settle in to squeal in peels of laughter at the same time.

Monkeys celebrate the calamity, thinking of it to be a new human circus.

Simi is left, holding her large hand-bag on the road, watching over the corpse of Kuber, as his body is disentangled from the car.

Sid, continues to watch sullenly, happy in one part to see his wife again, in body and spirit. 'She is the same, unchanged.'

'If only Sid was here, he would not think of this as justice. It seems to be God's revenge,' wishes Simi, as she crosses her heart.

Sid crosses his imaginary chest, over his sternum, and the clavicle's collar bone.

From the inner voice of Ray he speaks out loud, 'Jesus, have mercy, for they know not what they do.'

30. Hyperbole.

A figure of speech, whereby a statement is made emphatic by overstatement.

Illustration:
'I shall soar, I shall fly!'

30. The jump

Stanley had visited Sid's room the previous night before his demise at the cliff-hanger.

'I have signed off the documents on behalf of the fraudulent transfer that is being attempted by Kuber. Rather than making the Directorate of Settlement and Land Records have my name, I have signed on behalf of my sister, and my past mother, Tia. The ink used is as purchased by you from the old store behind the San Thorpe Museum, using the old paper of 1966. It is agreed in the sale deed, that Tia gifted the property to her maternal sister's daughter, Kajal who we all addressed as my sister Kaju. She and my mother were made the guardian for the land, and she is no more.'

'So Sir, Tia transacted the land to Kajal, your sister between 1968 and 1969, when your sister was born before in 1966. Tia passed away in the 1970s when you claim you were re-born.'

'Nothing else explains my dream. The precise location of the coins chest, the treasure's message by Tia, and the desire of Kuber to get me here. I must take the jump tomorrow.'

'Sir, but the treasure has been hidden below the land again by Kuber.'

'It is cursed in any case. I have no interest in a cursed treasure. It is luckier for all that it remains buried. Likewise, my sister will simply sell the land again to Kuber if she wishes, so she will be in the money, and Kuber Savla can have his treasure. He should have disclosed it to me, that he has usurped it, but anyway, neither Rekha nor Simi are interested in it.'

'So you let him keep it?'

'Well, he has the curses of so many women. Along with a cursed treasure. I wish him best of luck.'

'It is very clear Sir, that the old *Goa Cadestral* maps and land record has Tia's name. The computerization of all 12 taluka's of Goa was done after 1997, so as suggested by you, we will register this showing an old stamp duty document of 1991, when the Government of the day, had allowed each of the citizens of Goa to register their old documents. It can be managed by my *susegaad* friend Bombil and me.

'Stanley, you have done me a huge favour. Please send this old gift deed by registered post to my sister. I have emailed her the scanned copy. My wife has signed the no objection release deed document in Mumbai of my will, and is also a witness with my elder son who was born before 1997. I have used Kuber's frame work document, but changed the name to my sister for the land and done the signatures. Kuber wanted his name on the land transfer, and trusted me for this last step, as he knew my expertise in calligraphy and signatures, as well as finding authentic papers and ink. I had purchased the old London Museum's relics and Goa's stamps, when they were sold in an auction at the Buckingham Palace in 1999.'

'Hat's off to you sir. Your sister will bless you.'

'They are both the same. Kuber and my sister. Only one difference, one is more needy than the other, one more greedy than the other.'

'Kuber used to talk to me sir, late at night over drinks, that both your sisters Kajal and his sister Hema had a fate and destiny, intertwined like your mother Tanu and Tia. One was married to a dunce, the other to a scammer. It ate him up from inside always. He sought revenge, you have provided justice sir.'

'The passport for London is provided to you by Kuber sir himself. You know my son lives in Scotland. If you ever need, you have to write to him at his mailbox address and he will respond to you whether he is there or in the British Virgin Islands.

Sid woke up, a free man the next morning.

There was no estate left in his name.

He had executed his will and transferred most of his moveable assets to Simi's account already.

The immovable properties in London were willed to his son and his daughter and the Indian properties to his wife, who already had a share in them.

Now this Goa episode had come in as a bonus, and he really did not care about it as much. He thought of his sister perhaps daily, weekly, and worried, as much as their dad had.

The desire to fly was always there. He was born with it. 'I shall soar, I shall fly!' his soul over stated the facts to himself.

He had obtained a light suede and leathery winged costume from the apparatus of the Righteous Brothers in UK, an improved costume for para-sailing.

It had never been attempted to use on land, with wings.

When Kuber had invited him to the cliff hanging hangar, it was to show a spot, where helicopters could land for the hoi-polloi.

Little did he know that Sid would want to take Vaz's offer, to jump off the cliff, with ropes and harness tied to his jeep.

As the jeep began the tenacious journey uphill. Sid was supposed to run behind the jeep, and then take the gust of wind in the direction of the wind to scale new heights.

The initial soaring heights gave him an adrenaline rush he had not experienced for years. His wavy hair blew in bursts based on how much he turned. He could see Vaz the driver and his friend Kuber, wave out to him from below, a distance of perhaps few kilometres between them.

Then things started going wrong.

Suddenly, the ropes and harness from Kuber's side of the jeep snapped, as if the ropes had given way. Perhaps they were tampered with. It remained a mystery to Sid, while he was suspended in the sky.

The last Sid saw, was Vaz trying to gesticulate from outside the jeep, suspended as Sid was in thin air for a while. He had the view of the setting sun. It was a flaming crimson red. Perhaps dusk was prettier than dawn.

He could see Kuber, making no movement, no alarm at all, and no kind of concern, to re-adjust the harness or bring him in.

Sid could see Kuber, sitting as he did, having turned his back away from Sid, while Vaz trimmed the rope knots on the other side of the Jeep support as well.

Sid figured it was a setup.

It brought an end to the bonhomie, and Sid flew as much as he could with the parachute using the wind and the rope, set loose as he was over the deep sea.

For an initial few seconds, panic set in. Sid began talking to himself as he surveyed the beach below, and saw himself float toward a forested island ahead, that looked deserted.

Monkey Island.

Aside from trees swinging, he was unable to see any further.

The optimist in Sid awoke. He decided at the opportune time with tail winds, to flap his apparatus wings the bare minimum and simply glide. He would move his leg muscles just enough, to change direction.

The fall had slowed and he actually continued to fly for a few kilometres, as he drifted toward the forest, with the help of his tail fin and winged apparatus.

His friend's deed had been a blessing in disguise. It had allowed Sid to experience real flight. 'I wish I was a pilot, and had flown planes in this life.'

Perhaps, he could make it to monkey island if he flapped his wings a wee bit harder, and avoided the tree tops.

He could see the sand bar from atop, between the Palolem beach and the island.

There was the fable, that monkeys would jump and bounce atop turtles and head toward the island.

Perhaps it was a figment of his imagination.

'Or perhaps it's a clue from my past life?' he thought aloud to himself, as he stared into the setting sun.

'It could be the start anew to my next life.'

31. Epiphora

Is the repetition of the same word, or words at the end of successive phrases or sentences.

Illustration:
Some wanna remain
cut and dry
Dry
Dry
Why why?
I ask why?
...died
died.
...Cry
cry...
lied, lie
lied, lied.

31. Song of Sid and Ray's Ghost

I didn't create a hue and cry
When some chose to only lie
Ultimately we all gonna die
We all gonna die

As time elapses
Our friendship passes
Through hot and cold
And we all grow old
We all grow old
We all gonna die

Till we remain alive
How do we wanna live?
Some wanna remain cut and dry
Dry
Dry
Why why?
I ask why?
Some remain cut
Stuck in their own rut
Time has passed us by
So we have to say good bye

Then why cry?
Why cry?
Why lie?
Why not simply ask why?

End this I and my.
Mine is as much on the line,
For no reason nor rhyme
I don't care a dime.
Coz' you never even gave me a smile.
When I was gonna die,
Gonna die.

But I remain alive,
In my heart and soul.
Even though you do your falseness,
Spread the lies,
Completely break our ties.
I hate lies,
I hate your lies!
Even more,
Coz it was our bonhomie
And it only remained mine.
You broke away,
When you could have shared the loss
You allowed greed to gather moss
Your soul has died
That's why I could never succeed even when I tried.
I tried
Tried
Tried
So you were left to cry,
And cry!
Till I died and died.

We all gonna die,
So stop the lie
Stop the lie!
Else you will alone be left to cry,
To cry

Cry and Cry.

So stop the lie
Stop the lie!

You lied a lie
You lied
a lie.
You Lied and lied.

At least stop,
Stop living a lie,
Stop living a lie.

T h e E n d

Till the <u>next</u> re-incarnation.

The figures of speech preceding every chapter in the novel, are to be taken in the context of the story and their meaning in place in the narrative.

The story line is entirely fictional, but for some fool hardy 'figure of speeches' that a fool took from someone he called a friend.

Friendship is not merely expressed as figures of speech.

It commences with thought, and goes beyond the spoken word, and culminates in action and deeds.

A friend in deed, is a friend indeed
sun : jeev

The last word on Bogey.

Kabir was a mystic of the 1400-1500's. His contribution to poetry is legendary.

One of his *dohas*, struck me as a fledgling writer.

'dariya ki lehar dariyao hai ji'

The **river and its waves are one surf, there is no difference between the wave and the river. When the wave rises it is the water, and when it falls then too it is the same water**.

Where is the distinction?

Just as it is named as a wave, shall we not consider it to be water?

Isn't **friendship the same**?

We refer to its existence as camaraderie, bonhomie, and the presence of a friend, your bestie, as mate, L'ami/e, Amigo, at times even Lover, partner, etc...same with foes, fiends and enemies. What of those good friendships that turned sour, and went down the drain, into the same water?

The rise of the wave, is bonhomie and **fall of the wave in human psyche is a 'bogey bonhomie.'**

In recent years, your BFF is someone who has your back, someone you can trust, depend on. It is often centred around experiences, the past, the future in which there is togetherness and hope embellished in loyalty and intertwined faith in each other. There are many stories that are out there, displaying great sacrifices that pals may have made for each other and stood as examples for generations to come.

Rarely has a story been written about day to day pettiness in today's life and how it has percolated from the past; as to consider the impact of the continued association of the company someone keeps.

When bonhomie goes awry, relationships sour, and all hope is lost, the only silver lining in the grey clouds is the survival of those who live on, with memories, due to deeds done.

Hopefully all great pals, re-unite, if not in this life, then the next.

Just like the unfinished business of past lives, it may convert your friends to foes, an optimist hopes this reverses in re-birth.

May foes befriend each other.

In the bleak moments of betrayal, and the dawning of that information that a friend has discontinued you on social media, this story from the times of pre-e-commerce and pre-internet, showcases what bonhomie used to be. Today it has generally reduced to a like or a block or unfriending someone, yet secretly following news, gossip, and back-biting about the same person.

A majority of us has experienced this in some social group or the other.

Why?

Human nature!

People talk about those missing pals, whom they like or dislike. Strong extremities prompt conversations, rather than dull regular *J-i-joes*, who no one seems to notice. Someone with a learning disability, a stammer, a broke financial status, or a heartbreak, often slips by, and is weeded out of social groups, for want of time and intent, or both.

Are many friendships **causal**? Would you then classify them as **casual**? Or do some just deteriorate with passage of time? Lose flavour, or favour.

Often the people involved don't want to keep up. They have evolved or are simply no longer the same people anymore. A lot is happening to them.

Change, and change acceptance is hard with friends. You do not choose the family you are born in, but you somehow drift together as buddies.

Many make new friends easily. The introverts fall by the wayside, or develop hobbies and individual pastimes that do not need a crowd to mingle. Single is fine. Yet, most singles too, have a friend. At least one.

General social media research shows, that a person spends the maximum amount of time with their spouse, then the family and then children. Time with friends is usually in between all that. Thus the best friends are those you may find within your own family, where you can take your bonhomie to the grave, and hope they are standing around it, if not shedding a few tears.

Most regular friends and friendships look for social outings, share hobbies or some interest, even a relationship.

They may have grown up together in their youth, and grown apart in the same neighbourhood, or simply understand each others weakness and strengths. Someone you may have known for a long while, may no longer remain a friend, while those who strongly disagreed with you, were perceived to be 'in a different camp' come along just fine later.

That is the fraudulent reality of our times; friends don't know who is coming and who is going from their own life, for them to pick up the phone and say something to you- that could lead to a meet up and a healthy exchange of views.

This story you have read, is a pure work of fiction. Names, characters, and places are far from the reality to stretch the concept of 'Bogey' to it's entirety. As far from reality as Portugal today is from Goa. Most stories set in Goa, over romanticize Goa.

This story showcases a strong bond between friends, and everything that happens to them there, the good, the bad and the sinister.

This story is copyrighted material, and any re-production, or use of any part of it, in any form of print, publication, or imitation, can lead to infringement of my rights as an author.

So go, find your own story, find your own friends! I am sure they will do better, than the characters in this story, what Prahlad, Yug, Som, Kuber and Sid did to each other. Dinshaw being an exception. He had the power!

The author has had the mis-fortune, of experiencing some real fools as friends. Some whom he took on face value and some whom he really loves/loved. This story is dedicated to all those set of fools who call(ed) me a friend.

Sun:Jeev
May 7th 2024.

Quotes

' True friends stab you in the front.'

Oscar Wilde.

'The man of knowledge, must be able to not only love his enemies,

...but also hate his friends.'

Friedrich Nietzsche

'A friend in deed, is a friend indeed'

sun : jeev

sun:jeev 1st Novel

sun:jeev on a train ride to Goa, clicked by a friend (2013)

sun:jeev 2nd Novel

BOGEY BONHOMIE

This story is copyrighted material, and any re-production, or use of any part of it, in any form of print, publication, or imitation, can lead to infringement of my rights as an author.

sun:jeev

2024©Sanjeev Bhatia

Instagram
@sunjeevbhatia

Under copy right law in every nation, world wide rights for any electronic media / TV / Cable/ Broadcast/ Cinema / belong solely to the author.

sun:jeev 3rd Novel

Love is
NOT
Child's
PLAY

TRUTH & TIME, WAIT FOR NO ONE

Drama: a play for theatre

sun:jeev

'I have chosen the creative space of books. Like LP's vinyl return, some day the trend will be to read the stories of our generation.' **Sun:Jeev** (author)

<u>**B O G E Y BONHOMIE**</u> **This work is copyright of 2024 ©Sanjeev Bhatia:: ISBN: 9798863682747**

All rights reserved. No part of this work, covered by the copyrights hereon maybe reproduced or used in any form or by any means – graphic, electronic or mechanical, including photocopying, recording, taping, or information storage and retrieval systems, without prior written permission of the author.

Bogey Bonhomie©Copyright owned by sun:jeev
Cover design: Artist Preet Soni / Concept sun:jeev
Inside illustrations/images: Drishti Balani & sun:jeev.

Love is
N O T
Child's
P L A Y

TRUTH & TIME, WAIT FOR NO ONE

Drama - a play for theatre
sun:jeev

Manufactured by Amazon.ca
Bolton, ON